Three colleagues—
Three couples wh...
them. . .for love

'This is wrong,' Karen told Lee, her voice not nearly as firm as she wanted it to be.

'*Wrong*? How could it possibly be wrong?' he demanded roughly. 'Just to kiss, alone together, when we're both uncommitted elsewh—' Karen stared down—her vision a blur—and he rasped, cutting himself off. 'But you're *not*, are you? You're not free!'

Dear Reader

My starting point was the relationship between Nick and Helen in FULL RECOVERY. Thinking about their happy marriage, I started to wonder, What will come afterwards? Inevitably, circumstances change and there are challenges. As I wrote, I became intrigued by the characters of Megan and Karen and wanted to know what would come afterwards for them, too. In FULL RECOVERY Karen is swept off her feet by the wrong man. How does this affect her happiness later on with the right one? A GIFT FOR HEALING answers the question. And what about Megan? We know her in FULL RECOVERY as the Other Woman, but is it fair to dismiss her that way? Doesn't she deserve the right man too? I had to find him for her and then wrote MISLEADING SYMPTOMS to bring them together. All in all, I felt as much page-turning curiosity as any reader as this trilogy unfolded.

Lilian Darcy

A GIFT FOR HEALING is the second book of Lilian Darcy's Camberton Hospital trilogy. Look out for Megan in MISLEADING SYMPTOMS, the final book of the trilogy, in May 1997.

A GIFT FOR HEALING

BY
LILIAN DARCY

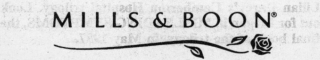

MILLS & BOON®

First published in Great Britain 1997
Harlequin Mills & Boon Limited,
Eton House, 18-24 Paradise Road, Richmond, Surrey TW9 1SR

© Lilian Darcy 1997

ISBN 0 263 80076 8

Set in Times 10 on 11 pt. by
Rowland Phototypesetting Limited
Bury St Edmunds, Suffolk

03-9704-51946-D

Printed and bound in Great Britain
by Mackays of Chatham PLC, Chatham

CHAPTER ONE

'KAREN GRAHAM, please.' The voice on the phone was abrupt, gravelly, male and exceedingly impatient.

Lee Shadwell's immediate impulse, at a quarter to one on an unusually busy Monday, was to be abrupt, impatient and equally male and tell the unknown caller to get knotted.

He restrained himself, however, and was about to offer instead the option of taking Mr Impatience's number and getting Sister Graham to phone him back when he remembered that he'd just glimpsed her on his way past the patients' dining-room, still helping Old Mrs Ruppert with her lunch when all the other patients had finished and gone.

Karen herself was fifteen minutes late on a lunch-break which, even on good days, rarely managed to achieve the prescribed hour.

So, instead, he asked rather crisply, 'Is this personal?'

'Is that any of your business?' came a barked retort.

Again restraint came with an effort, and Lee drawled, 'As manager of this place, it just might be. If this is work-related, I may be able to help you instead.'

'Well, it's not. Can I speak to her, or can't I? It's important.'

An irate parent? Lee wondered. It didn't sound like a young man's voice. 'As it happens, she's overdue for lunch and I can get her for you,' he offered. 'Now, would you like to hold or ring back? It may be a few minutes.'

'I'll hold. I've already been cut off once, getting transferred from the front desk or God knows where.'

'Very well, sir,' Lee responded through gritted teeth.

The fact that he frequently encountered rudeness in his managerial role didn't seem to help in dealing with this fellow. The man had his back up and his blood boiling, and Lee pressed the button that would hold the caller on line two with unnecessary force. Hopefully Karen would give the man short shrift, even if he was her father. Or a bullying older brother, perhaps. . .? He realised, and wasn't entirely happy about the fact, that he didn't know anything about her personal circumstances.

Striding along the lengthy corridor to the dining-room, he saw that Mrs Ruppert had finished at last. A wing of Karen Graham's softly waved blonde hair swung forward to hide her face as she patted the old lady gently on the shoulder and said, 'Well done! Once I'd cut the meat for you you did it all yourself, didn't you?'

There was a crow of pleasurable agreement from Mrs Ruppert, although she spoke no intelligible words. The victim of a stroke several months ago, her rehabilitation had been disappointing in this area. Karen continued, 'Now, do you remember what we practised this morning about transferring you from your chair to your walking-frame? Gaye Wyman is going to help you with that. Do you remember Gaye? She's the physiotherapist who spent some time with you yesterday.'

'Just finishing my tea and my notes, Mrs Ruppert,' came an energetic voice, and Lee realised for the first time that Karen and the elderly patient were not alone in the dining-room.

The realisation was cause for a little concern as Gaye was not what anyone would call small in stature or insignificant in bearing. How had neat, contained Sister Graham managed to overshadow her in his perception?

Brushing the question aside, he stepped inside the door and said quickly, 'Personal phone call for you, Karen. On hold, in my office.'

'Oh. Right. Um. . .'

'I'll take over, Karen,' Gaye said cheerfully. 'You're late for your break already, aren't you?'

The blonde day sister glanced up at the electric wall clock. 'Ten to one? Par for the course, I'm afraid.' It was said without resentment. 'Thanks, Lee.'

She said goodbye to Mrs Ruppert, giving her another pat, then hurried towards the door and fell into step beside Lee. 'Mrs Ruppert is doing much better already,' she told him as soon as they were safely out of the patient's earshot. Mrs Ruppert's hearing was deceptively acute, unimpaired by the stroke which had left her speech in tatters.

'Missing Mr Ruppert?' Lee asked.

'Definitely. And worried about his hospital stay.' The elderly woman's husband, who was her sole carer, was in hospital this week himself for a fairly minor procedure, which was why Mrs Ruppert had had to come here. 'Although it may turn out to be a blessing in disguise as it gives us a very good chance to assess her abilities.'

'That was my thought, yes. What's your impression so far, then?'

'Well, it's clear that she could do more than she is doing if she had someone who knew how to give her the right help.'

Lee clicked his tongue. 'If she's improved in the few days she's been with us, I expect you're right. But she did go through rehab, didn't she? After the stroke?'

'Yes, but I imagine the problem is him, not her. He doesn't know how to motivate her; doesn't know how much to expect and demand from her in terms of self-care. That's all just guesswork on my part, really. The home assessment wasn't as detailed as it could have been. Although, apparently, Mr Ruppert has rejected the option of day hospital for his wife in the past.'

'Let's see if we can keep her in for another week, then,' Lee proposed, 'and have Mr Ruppert come to our skills group. He may change his thinking.'

'Could we keep her in?' Karen's response was eager. 'Do we have a bed for her?'

'I can find one.' With a little juggling. Something he'd become adept at.

'What, there's a spare lying somewhere in a cupboard under the sink?' she teased. 'Or you'll bring a blow-up rubber mattress?'

'Be handy, wouldn't it, if that was all "a bed" involved?' he agreed with a laugh as they reached the office.

She hadn't been thinking about the phone call at all, he realised, which was proof—if he had still needed any in the six weeks Karen Graham had been working here—that her concern for their patients was genuine. Now she frowned a little with her delicate drawn brows as she picked up the instrument and murmured, 'I wonder who. . .?' Then she broke off to say, 'Hello?' There was clearly no response at the other end, and she looked puzzled.

'It's on silent hold,' Lee remembered. 'Do you want me to leave, by the way? He said it was personal.' Again he was confident in his judgement of her: she wasn't the type to abuse the privilege of personal calls.

'No, no,' she replied quickly, hovering over the phone console. 'But how do I—?'

'Press line two.'

'Aha!' She did so. 'Hello, Karen Graham speaking. . .' That clear, sweet voice had been catching Lee's ear with rather delightful frequency of late. Then there was an abrupt change of tone and manner as her expression tightened with shock. '*Paul. . .!*'

Feeling her hungry stomach lurching and churning with unpleasant violence, Karen instinctively turned away from the desk and swivel chair where Lee Shadwell's rather impressive frame was now twisting as he reached for some papers. 'How. . .how did you find me?'

'I managed,' Paul Chambers drawled, the understated irony a typical product of his cynical intelligence.

'What do you want? It's been. . .nearly three months.'

She wanted to find some way of saying it all less bluntly, intensely aware as she was of Lee at his desk behind her. She heard the faint, fluid scratch of his fountain-pen on paper and knew that, even if his syrupy dark-blond head was bent over the knotty administrative work which took up so much of his time, he could hardly help hearing her abrupt, shocked questions just feet away. But there was no way to mince around any of this, hearing Paul's voice like that out of the blue.

She added deliberately, if shakily, 'I meant it when I said I never wanted to see you again. I still mean it.'

'I'm in hospital.'

Even though she knew by this time the starkness of his words would have been quite deliberate, she still felt the knife-thrust of alarm and drew in a quick, hissing breath. 'In hospital? Where?'

'Here. Camberton. Chest ward. Same as before.'

'But, Paul, your last tests were still clear. Just three months ago. What went wrong?'

He laughed harshly. 'Haven't been looking after myself properly, have I? Since you left me—'

'*Don't* try to pin that on me!' she came in, her tone cold, meaning it. 'I won't take that responsibility any more. I can't!' The painful failure of it all swept her once again and she totally forgot Lee Shadwell's presence. 'I tried to before, and you—you didn't—'

At the other end of the phone Paul shifted his tack and she wondered, as she had wondered so often before, if this mood was genuine. 'Look, I'm not expecting anything,' he said quietly—tiredly. 'I just thought you'd want to know. They want to do a contact tracing, you see, in case I've zapped anyone else with the dreaded bug and—'

This was a ruse, she now knew. Concerned herself about the possibility of disease, she had had two chest X-rays over the past six months—one just after the heady beginning of their relationship, and the other nearly three months ago immediately after its traumatic end. Both had proved clear and her last short letter to Paul, after she returned to England, had informed him of this. She didn't have TB then, and she hadn't seen him since. There was no need for him to mention her name in connection with a contact tracing, and he knew it.

And yet she didn't attack him on the issue, but said instead with real concern, 'How bad is it, Paul? Your relapse?'

There was an efficient, masculine movement behind her and Lee Shadwell got up from his desk, muttering something about 'chasing up the planning committee's report on. . .' He left the room without finishing the sentence, and she knew that he had only left in order to give her some privacy. As busy as he was he couldn't afford this exile from his office and she bit her lip, knowing that she had to end the conversation with Paul as soon as she possibly could.

'They caught it early,' he was saying. 'I stayed on in Morocco for about two months after you. . .left. I've been back in England for a few weeks. Guess the symptoms started around then. I was feeling pretty wretched, and I didn't—'

'I can't talk now, Paul,' she interrupted, torn three ways between anger, reluctance and that strange pull on her that Paul had once exercised at will. 'I'm sorry.'

There was a silence, then he said, 'God, you ask me how I feel, but when I—'

'I'm at work, as you know. In the manager's office,

and he. . .needs the phone,' she improvised. It was probably true.

'OK. Fine. I guess that's it, then. Just thought you'd want to know. . .'

'Paul, I—'

But he had quietly hung up, with that impeccable timing which left her feeling that *she* was the one who had been unfair, inconsiderate and badly behaved.

Turning to replace her own receiver, she swore half under her breath—using a string of epithets that had figured daily in Paul's conversation. Ugly words, ugly sounds, and she was sorry she'd let them slip—especially when there was a sound behind her and she whirled clumsily to find Lee's frame filling the doorway, his gold-flecked brown eyes fixed on her with an unreadable look and the smooth bow of his mouth steady and unsmiling.

Had he heard her profanity? For some reason the thought that he might have done made her feel worse even than she had felt on the phone with Paul. She didn't normally let fly so foully, and she didn't want Lee Shadwell to think that she was the kind of person who did.

'I'm so sorry, Lee,' she told him quickly, flushing, and left him to his work.

Going to the small staff-room to retrieve the packet of sandwiches, fruit and cake that she had brought from home, Karen saw with relief that the May sunshine still shone brightly outside as it had just begun to do when she arrived shortly before seven this morning. Last week she had found a little suntrap of a nook on the south side of the building, screened from view by young shrubs and warmed by the wall of Yorkshire stone behind which was the furnace and electrical system.

Most of the other staff seemed to favour the designated retreat, where they could brew a cup of tea or heat food in a microwave, but Karen gladly exchanged convenience for fresh air and privacy today.

She put a small plastic cloth on the grass to protect her dark blue uniform from damp and sat down, with the view of Camberton spread out before her. The larger buildings of the city centre were hidden from view in the distance by trees and hillside, but she could see the hospital a mile away and the new tracts of housing beyond. Their gardens were beginning to grow nicely now, softening the rawness they had had when first built several years ago.

This place, Linwood Gardens Day Hospital and Respite Care Centre—its first phase of construction less than a year old—still had that raw look and the 'Gardens' part of the name still owed more to the planner's model than it did to fact. Still, with spring here now and gardeners at work today on the sloping grounds that led down to the stone gate, greenery would soon fill the place in.

'. . .soon fill the place in.' She repeated the thought aloud, but she was fooling herself if the thought that her focus really lay in the area of landscaping.

Is Paul trying to get me to come back to him? she wondered. Is that what his call was really about? I'll have to go and see him in hospital. I owe him that much. But nothing more, surely, and I'll say it to him again if I have to. He mustn't think that there's any chance. I made that clear on the phone. . .

The phone. With Lee Shadwell in the background, trying gallantly not to listen. Somehow the fact that he had been there as an unwilling audience made Paul's phone call a far more disturbing thing than it would otherwise have been. She couldn't help trying to conjure up what she'd said, examining her words from Lee's point of view.

What must he think of me? was the question that

drummed persistently in her head. She realised for the first time that her six weeks in this job, hard at first as she had tried to put her dramatic months of living with Paul into the past, had been made immeasurably easier by the unstated confidence Lee Shadwell had shown in her work and her character almost from the beginning.

Would that be shattered now? It was a disastrous possibility.

She saw a movement out of the corner of her eye, thought at first that it was a gardener and then realised that the man's clothing was far too well tailored and it was Lee himself, brushing through the shrubbery to reach her.

'So you've discovered my favourite haunt, too, I see?' he drawled, and she started to scramble to her feet at once, flushing and feeling for the second time that day like an insensitive intruder on his privacy.

'I'll go elsewhere if you want to be alone,' she offered.

But he held out a hand. 'Sit! Stay! I didn't mean that at all. I've been looking for you, and Heather said she'd seen you go outside. Just wanted to tell you to take your time. You were late off. Don't feel you need to be back on board till two if you need the time.'

'I'm fine,' she told him, flushing again.

He was clearly referring to her conversation with Paul, and once again she wondered what he had made of all those dramatic phrases. His gold-flecked gaze caught hers for a moment and she thought, He's not going to probe, is he? I couldn't bear to talk about it—to have him know.

Although why *that* should be the case. . .

'Just thought you might,' was all he said, then he turned from her to look at the view. 'Much nicer than a stuffy staff-room, isn't it?'

'Much. But, if it's your spot, I won't—'

'Cut that out!' he said impatiently. 'I might have

known you'd take it that way, and I didn't mean it like that at all. I haven't managed to escape to this little retreat since last summer, actually, what with the workload, but if we ever do end up here together. . .'

'We can swap sandwiches and make a picnic of it,' she finished, sensing the teasing direction of his words, and he smiled.

The boyishness of the expression was quite deliberate and positively evil in intent. No man in his thirties, and capably built to boot, should be able to look so poignantly waif-like!

'What *are* those—just out of interest?' he asked.

Karen's capitulation was immediate. 'Curried egg and lettuce on granary bread. Then there's a banana, and—'

'On second thoughts, don't tell me! I sneaked a bowl of Double Sugar-Frosted Krunchy-Wunchies from the kitchens at half past nine this morning, and haven't managed anything since.'

'Double Sugar-Frosted Krunchy-Wunchies?'

'Perhaps I've taken a few liberties with the name,' he conceded, 'but it's what they tasted like. The best part was the milk. . .and I think it was on the turn.'

She groaned. 'You're like my old dog at home, fixing me with her big brown eyes and saying, "I haven't eaten for a week, honestly!"'

'No. No, I really couldn't. Not one of your curried egg and lettuce sandwiches. Not even *half* a one. . .' He was still doing it quite deliberately.

'Here.' She sighed in mock exasperation and handed half the sandwich across and he downed it with great relish, followed by a satisfied grin, in under a minute.

'I'll pay you back,' he assured her seriously. 'I know there's another full packet of Double Sugar-Frosted Krunchy-Wunchies still around somewhere. . .'

'Can't wait!'

Then, just when she was expecting him to leave, he

dropped into an easy squat—rocking lightly on his toes and resting his forearms casually across his thighs—and she thought, So supple and fit, compared to our patients! Compared to me, for that matter. I didn't keep myself in shape very well when I was with Paul. . .

But he was speaking again. 'So you have a greedy but well-beloved old dog at home, do you?'

'Yes, I—'

She stopped, caught by a sudden, unexpected gush of sadness. Did she have a dog? Certainly not now in her small flat. But was dear old Lucy even still alive? It was more than six months since she'd hardened her heart against making contact with that house near Hampstead Heath where Lucy lived. . .with her own parents and two younger brothers.

She had sent one brief postcard at Christmas to let them know that she was all right, but had deliberately avoided giving a return address. Too many harsh words had been spoken on both sides during that awful scene in October. . .

She couldn't tell Lee all that, though, so she went on carefully, 'I have a dog. Sixteen now. Her name's Lucy and, yes, she's terminally greedy but very loving and really doesn't disturb me *much* when she sleeps right in the middle of my bed. There's usually a good four inches left on either side for me.' Then the quick admission, 'She lives in London. I haven't seen her for. . .a while.'

'With your parents?'

'Yes.'

There was a cloud shadow travelling towards them. She could see it, diving over the roof of the main building at Camberton Hospital and sliding its blue-grey shade over the trees and streets and houses. Over the new green lawns of Linwood Gardens now. . .and, yes, the day had darkened a little, the temperature had dropped and they were in shade.

'I'd better go in,' Lee said, the deliberate boyishness gone now. He looked just what he was—the capably intelligent manager of this expanding institution, and very largely responsible for its success.

She felt again, and more strongly, the determination that he should know nothing about Paul. It would be disastrous to lose his professional respect, which she surely would if he knew how carelessly she had opened herself to scandal. And with Paul again in Camberton Hospital with multi-drug-resistant tuberculosis. . .

She shuddered. Lee Shadwell must not know!

'I imagine the phone's ringing its head off,' he was saying. 'Do take the time you're supposed to have, won't you? No sense my new day sister fretting herself into the ground quite yet!'

'Thanks, Lee. I. . . You really don't have to worry that that will happen.'

There was a little too much intensity in her assurance and his glance fixed on her, narrowing in surprised assessment for a moment. His lips parted and the tip of his tongue touched his white teeth in preparation for speech, but then he appeared to dismiss the issue and simply rose and lifted a hand in casual salute.

Karen watched him as he ducked down to the wheel-chair access ramp that led up to the main entrance, thinking for no good reason about how well that plain white shirt and the dark, tailored trousers suited his masculine grace and pale gold tan.

The cloud passed on to bring sunshine again and, just before he disappeared from view, the light caught at his hair, making the straight strands on top look like threads of white gold against the myriad shades of golden toffee and darker treacle beneath. No wonder the patients seemed to love him on sight—everyone from the frail old ladies of the north wing to the south wing's wheel-chair-bound children. . .

Karen ate the rest of her sandwiches. Lee had really only filched a quarter of the generous packet she'd made at six-thirty this morning. The bread was still fresh and tasty, the lettuce crisp and the egg nicely spiced. And yet she might have been eating Lee's ludicrously named cereal for all the pleasure she took in her lunch.

The dog, Lucy. . .her brothers. . .her parents. . .Paul.

It was seven months since that appalling scene in London when her mother had said with a stone-hard face and bitter voice, 'Go with him, then, since you love him so deeply; since you think it such an honour to be a piece of baggage for him to cart around the globe for a few months till he's tired of you. I thought we'd brought you up to have more sense, more decency. . .'

'Pamela—' But her father hadn't been given a chance to placate his wife or plead for his daughter.

'I can't understand why *you* aren't saying this, Reg! She's only known this man a few weeks, and he cares so little about her that he's prepared to—'

'He *does* care!' Karen had cried, red stains burning on her cheeks. 'You can't measure the growth of that in units of time. He needs me. He couldn't go on without me. He loves me! He's told me so.'

'It's sex, I suppose.'

'It's not! That's only a tiny—'

'Oh, *leave*! Just leave, Karen, before I—' A ragged, angry sob. 'And don't come back. You say you're doing this with your eyes open and that it's your life. Well, let it be your life, then! I want no more part of it.'

'All right.' Head held high. 'Let's have it that way. I hoped you'd understand that love. . .comes in different packages sometimes. But if you don't. . .'

She stormed out, with tears of rage and pride stinging her eyes. 'Let it be your life. . .I want no more part of it,' her mother had said and would be taken at her bitter word, Karen vowed in her anger. She would prove to herself that her mother was wrong. She would prove to the world that love could grow and deepen and become ever richer without that pretty piece of legal sanctification, the marriage certificate, that Paul was so cleverly scathing about. . .

Only her love *hadn't* been equal to the challenges it faced. It hadn't grown and become richer. It took just three months of living with him in Morocco to strip the scales from her eyes, and if she had thought Paul cleverly scathing about the institution of marriage it was nothing to how cleverly scathing he could be on the subject of their own relationship.

He jeered at her notions of love and sacrifice, compromise, sharing and support. He mocked her romantic gestures; greedily absorbed every bit of energy she had expended on him; used her savings on extravagances for himself while she was slaving at home in their outdated Moroccan kitchen, cooking meals for him that—many times—he did not bother to show up for.

And when she demanded his respect and consideration he laughed knowingly, telling her that she loved the sacrifices she made for him and would be lost without him.

Twice he realised that he had gone too far, and there was a scene of such regret and humility from him that she found excuses for his terrible behaviour—his illness, adjusting to each other, the vital work that was his writing, her inability to match his sharp, cynical mind in conversation.

Then, after more subtle trampling on her feelings, he bought her flowers and a dress on Valentine's Day and took her to dinner at the best restaurant in Tangiers, and she went through the evening with the strangest feeling of detachment—from him, from the whole scene, even from herself.

She saw the secret, satisfied smile on his face, listened to the casual, almost absent-minded compliments and endearments, felt his urgent, clumsy caresses and thought, He thinks I'm a puppet and that he controls the strings. He thinks I'm hooked by all this, and I was, at first. I trusted his sincerity. I thought these things were gestures of love and giving. But they're not. They're gestures of manipulation and control, deliberate from the very beginning. He thinks this evening will pay for another three months of my devotion. But he's wrong.

The next day, after another horrible scene—strange, when scenes were very foreign to her nature—she packed her things, took the thin packet of her remaining traveller's cheques and returned to England.

She thought of going to her parents, and frankly admitting her terrible mistake and telling them how much she had learned from it, but then hardened her heart once more. To face a tirade of I-told-you-sos from a mother who had been so quick to repudiate her? No!

Karen didn't intend to return to Camberton permanently, but seeking refuge with her old friend Susie, a nurse at the hospital, led to a weekly flip through the job listings in nursing magazines and this one caught her eye.

Having spent a year as a staff nurse in a nearby nursing home before moving to Camberton's male chest ward, where she had been made ward sister after three and a half years, and being able to provide glowing references from three years of volunteer work in recreational therapy for the aged and handicapped as a teenager, she obtained the position of day sister here.

And, Lee's generous injunction to take her time notwithstanding, if she didn't get back to her post soon the whole establishment might well fall down around her ears!

She screwed her sandwich and cake wrappings into a ball and threw them into the bin outside the main entrance as she reviewed the afternoon routine.

Day-patient activities should finish at a quarter to three

to allow time for toileting before carers or minibuses arrived to transport Linwood's thirty adult day patients home between three and three-fifteen.

At three-forty-five the twelve physically or mentally impaired children currently in residence for up to four weeks of respite care would return from their day schools. She herself was due to leave at four, but often ended up staying later to tie off the loose ends she hadn't managed to get to during the day.

A group of Linwood's elderly patients had gone on a sandwich picnic today to Camberton's small but very pretty botanical gardens, and were due to return at any moment. In fact. . . Yes, here was the bus, pulling in now.

Part-time recreational therapist Louise Brown, a junior nurse and a volunteer carer had accompanied the fourteen patients, and Karen knew that they would probably be glad of her assistance at this point so she stopped to wait by the covered entrance.

Louise saw her there and leaned out of the just-opened bus door to say cheerily, 'It went very well.'

'Good.'

'Although Mr Standish is having some chest pain now and he forgot his angina pills, so I'm sending Julie inside with him straight away.' She stepped aside, to let the elderly man pass on the arm of the younger nurse. He looked a little agitated and upset, Karen noticed. 'As to further details,' Louise went on, 'I'll fill you in in a minute, shall I, when we've got them all safely inside?'

'Sounds good. I'll give a hand from here.'

The cement kerb had been made deliberately high at this point so that there was no big step for stiff, frail old limbs to negotiate. It helped a lot and soon, one at a time, each patient had walked down the aisle of the bus and was safely on the ground.

Each patient, that is, except Mrs Tostell.

Louise and Karen exchanged a glance. She wasn't

asleep. Far from it. She was staring straight ahead and waiting with stubborn, exaggerated impatience for her problem, whatever it was, to be noticed.

Familiar with this difficult day patient, Karen prompted gently, 'Aren't you coming out, Mrs Tostell?'

'No.' Her small mouth shut like a sharp little trap as she finished the syllable.

'Is there a problem?'

'I've hurt my ankle.'

'When did you do that, Mrs Tostell? You didn't say anything,' Louise Brown pointed out patiently.

'No one noticed. I fell. And I had to get up all by myself because no one was there. You were all just sitting and jabbering by the fountain! The flooring in that conservatory is a disgrace!'

'You'd better take everyone else in,' Karen said to Louise in an aside. 'If she is injured—and she's frail in spite of her good mobility, so she probably is—then it's a nursing matter.'

'Right, then,' Louise agreed, then added candidly, 'Rather you than me!' Their regular bus driver, Mac Daley, who was still sitting in his seat behind the wheel, rolled his eyes in agreement.

'She's been alternately griping and playing the martyr all afternoon,' Louise went on. 'We'd got a nice little spontaneous reminiscence session going over the spring bulbs, and Mr Standish was telling us the sweetest story about his wife who died last year when Mrs Tostell spoiled the whole mood by insisting on— Anyway, can't tell you it all now but I'm sure that's what got the old pet's angina going.'

'Never mind. I'll just get up, then, and come down the steps by myself,' Mrs Tostell was saying with bitter heroism. 'I expect I'll be able to manage without too much pain.'

'No, please, Mrs Tostell,' Karen said, going quickly

along the aisle to where she was seated in the third row. 'Let me look at your ankle first. Which one is it?'

'Well, the one that's all swollen and purple, of course!'

Actually, the injury was barely perceptible, and Karen couldn't feel any displacement of the bone when she prodded gently with her fingers. There was a sharp hiss from Mrs Tostell, though, and with old bones the loss of calcium made them prone to injury. It could well be a fracture.

'I'm going to get you a wheelchair, Mrs Tostell,' she said. 'Please don't try to move. I'll be back as soon as I can.'

She hurried inside and got a wheelchair from the bay next to Reception, where there were always a couple stored, and had soon helped an ostentatiously stoical Mrs Tostell out of the bus and into the chair.

The elderly woman needed the toilet, understandably, and after this was accomplished Karen took her to the lounge, where some card games were in progress.

Lee was in his office, and frowned when she told him what had happened. 'She should be X-rayed, then.'

'I think so. She's a difficult old thing in many ways, but not one to amplify a minor pain. . .although she's certainly playing this for all the guilt she can get. If it *is* broke Louise will never hear the end of it, for not noticing the fall.'

'And why didn't she?' he frowned again.

'Because Mrs Tostell had left the group without telling anyone, as I understand it. They were all chatting about the past, and she hates that.'

'Yes,' he agreed. 'It runs quite deep, too. I'm beginning to wonder about it since for so many old people reminiscence is such a pleasure. Anyway, the ankle is the immediate issue, not her problems with the past. I have to go over to the hospital myself for a planning meeting in half an hour.' He looked at his watch, and amended ruefully, 'Twenty minutes. Time's on skates today. So I'll run her up there myself. If you could let her daughter know to meet her there instead of coming here. . .'

On the phone Mrs Tostell's daughter, Judith was sensible about the whole thing. 'She didn't say anything till she got back? I'm not surprised. She's so determined not to make a fuss at first, and then her resolve breaks down and it's more trouble than if she'd fussed in the first place. Still, if it's just a hairline fracture she's got off lightly. . .and so have I! I'll be at the hospital as soon as I can.'

Fifteen minutes later Karen helped Lee to make Mrs Tostell comfortable in the front passenger seat of the staff car he used. Hearing a stiff, sour little account of the accident from the difficult old lady, his response was courteous and good-humoured.

'It's hard when there's something going on that you don't want to take part in, isn't it? Perhaps you could let one of the staff know on your next outing if you'd like to do something different. Someone could have helped you.'

'I'm not a toddler who needs to be with a responsible adult at all times.'

'True,' he conceded gravely. 'But you did fall, Mrs Tostell. Nurse Martin could have given you a walking-frame.'

'Hmm!'

Karen caught Lee's eye as he took his seat behind the wheel. They were in for an interesting ride! But she liked the way he didn't talk down to people like Mrs Tostell and knew that, in spite of her prickliness, the elderly woman preferred straight talk to simpering and cute humour.

'Will you be back?' Karen asked him.

'Probably not. I'm expecting it to go on until after five. They want my input on the next stage in the construction of this place, and I've got a few contentious points to make! Refer any problems to Alison or Peter.'

'They'll thank me for that!' she quipped. The latter was Linwood's financial administrator, while the former was the deputy nursing manager who worked from one until nine in the evenings to oversee the sometimes difficult task of preparing the in-patients—up to thirty of them—for bed.

Lee gave a last smile. He had a very open smile—very male, that frankness, somehow—with a teasing quality to it that she liked. Then it faded suddenly as he looked at his left hand.

'Now, what on earth is this that I'm holding?' he muttered. It was a long white envelope. 'Damn! Mr Standish gave it to me and wanted it put somewhere for safe-keeping. He's had to lie down. Can you. . .?'

'Of course.' Karen took the envelope and Lee drove off, his mind already leaping ahead to his meeting—if that abstracted frown was any guide.

After putting Mr Standish's envelope in a file tray on Lee's desk Karen returned to her work. By now she was running a little behind schedule so that it was twenty past four when she got away for the day. As predicted Lee hadn't returned from his meeting, although Mrs Tostell's daughter had phoned to report that there was indeed a hairline fracture and that a sturdy support bandage had been applied.

'Does this mean she'll have to stay home from day hospital until it's better?' Judith Grey had wanted to know. Karen had detected the anxiety behind the question.

'Let's hope not,' she'd said cautiously. 'We'll have to let you know.'

Twenty past four. The sun was still shining, and Karen was tired. So much so that when her Number 34 bus came past the stop at the bottom of the hill when she was only halfway down she couldn't be bothered to run for it and let it roar on, without even trying to catch the driver's attention. A twenty-minute wait would follow now. Unless. . .

Paul. There had been the business of Mrs Tostell's ankle and then Mr Standish's angina, which hadn't fully subsided as it should have done after he'd dissolved a nitroglycerin pill under his tongue. In the end they'd sent him up to the hospital too, and he'd been admitted overnight for observation.

There had also been half a dozen more small, typical difficulties during the course of the afternoon, and she hadn't had a chance to think very much about that disturbing phone call she'd received at lunchtime. Now it all came flooding back and in her mind's eye she saw Lee's concerned, steady, and not entirely readable gaze once again.

I should get it over with, or it will just nag at me, she thought. But not today, surely! I can't face it today.

And yet, when she reached the bus-stop and saw a Number 17 Camberton Hospital bus just fifty yards away, she didn't hesitate and raised her hand to signal the driver.

It would be odd and. . .difficult to see Paul again.

CHAPTER TWO

THE men's chest ward assaulted Karen with its familiar combination of sights, sounds and smells. Knowing how much living she had done and how much she'd changed since the time she had worked here, Karen had half expected to see a totally new roster of faces amongst the staff.

But she had only left about seven months ago and there was Staff Nurse Lindsay Watson behind the desk at the nurses' station, as well as Pat Conister—who had been promoted to Sister when Karen herself had left. As she entered the ward she saw along the corridor the blonde bell of hair belonging to Dr Megan Stone, senior registrar in thoracic medicine, and even one of the middle-aged patients in the small lounge looked familiar.

Going up to the desk, she braced herself for a curious round of questions from Lindsay and Pat but it didn't happen.

'We heard from Susie that you were back,' Lindsay said.

There was a tiny silence. 'If it's Paul Chambers you've come to see. . .' Pat hesitated.

'Yes. It is,' Karen answered steadily.

Pat and Lindsay were both nice and not prone to vicious scandalmongering, but she knew that her decision last year to leave the hospital and go to Morocco with Paul as his lover had ignited a wildfire of gossip throughout the hospital—and they were no more immune to curiosity on the subject than anyone else. Opinion had been deeply divided. Shocking? Sordid? Romance of the century?

26

He hadn't been her patient at the time. Scrupulously she had waited until his discharge before going to him, but it was a distinction in name only. She had known within two weeks of his admission that she would give herself to him if he wanted her. Did Pat and Lindsay think that the scandal was going to erupt all over again? She couldn't afford to care.

'He's in bed 9,' Lindsay offered.

'I know.' The room had been fitted up to provide complete respiratory isolation last time he had been in here, with negative air-flow from the corridor to the exhaust fans in the windows. She wondered if any other patients had needed those strict precautions since.

'He'll be pleased to see you,' Pat suggested, but it was a meaningless comment and Karen resisted any desire to talk longer.

'I haven't got a lot of time, so. . .'

'Go ahead, then.'

As she approached the room she could already hear the two nurses, whispering behind her.

'Paul. . .?' Her voice sounded very odd through the particulate respirator, which staff were required to wear in his room, and she knew that she would look even odder.

He was in bed, and his eyes were closed when she entered. She might even have disturbed him from sleep because he looked very disorientated for several seconds as he opened them. Then. . .

'Karen!' A hoarse cry, and his face lit up. 'I. . .I didn't think you'd come.'

His voice cracked, and Karen felt as if her stomach was filled with a stone. He looked terrible. His handsome, leonine face was haggard and ashen and tired, and his big, masculine frame slumped like a sack in the bed.

Have I done this to him? was her instant thought, then she rebelled against it. He had done that to *her* from the beginning—blackmailing her emotionally into taking responsibility for his well-being, and then blaming her for his own sabotage of her efforts to care for him. She *wasn't* going to be hurt or taken in by that manipulation again! This visit wouldn't be happening at all if she hadn't been weighed down by a sense of duty and honour which, she was starting to suspect, was a little too deeply ingrained for her own good.

She said carefully, 'I came to see if there was anything you needed. Anything I could do, or bring for you. Books! Is your house being kept up? I could—'

'Books would be good. . . And my house?' The small stone terrace house he had inherited from his mother, and in which he and Karen had lived together for two weeks, before seeking the sun in North Africa. 'No, I hadn't managed to evict the tenants before I had to come in here. I've been in a hostel.'

'A *hostel*? What sort of hostel? Where?'

'Well, a hotel,' he admitted. 'One of those smallish B and B places.'

There! She'd caught him out already in an attempt to milk her sympathy, by dramatising his circumstances.

'Most of those places tend to be pretty nice,' she told him coolly.

'Yes, it wasn't bad. . .'

She stayed for almost an hour, feeling the minutes drag horribly and finding the respirator increasingly claustrophobic. He had two bad attacks of coughing, and she discovered to her dismay that he'd been here for nearly two weeks already. 'Not responding too well to the drugs so far,' he told her. 'My general fitness was down. I hadn't managed to look after myself—'

Don't try to blame me for that! She didn't say the words aloud, but her set face must have betrayed her repudiation because he didn't finish the sentence. And five minutes later when she tried to talk about his writ-

ing—the book about homelessness and disease in New
York City that he had been working on—he was sneering
at her for her 'crass perceptions and mediocre mind'.

'Write down the list of books you want me to get for
you,' she told him baldly, ignoring his put-down. It had
lost the power to hurt her now. 'And I'll get as many of
them as I can and leave them at the desk for you. And
anything else you need.'

'Then you're not coming again?'

'Are you surprised?'

'I've been a bastard to you, haven't I?'

'You said it.'

'Karen, I— It's because I—'

'Don't, Paul,' she said through clenched teeth. 'Just
write the list, and don't worry about the cost.'

With the mask almost suffocating her by the time she
had waited for him to write the laborious list, she left at
last and tore the respirator from her face—totally drained
by the encounter and vowing not to come back. She owed
him nothing, surely!

It was cool outside now and gloriously fresh—a life-
saving blast of air that she drank in as if it were cold
mountain spring water, desperate to rid herself of the
mood of her meeting with Paul which clung to her like
some musty miasma of dust.

It was half past five and all that lay ahead for the
evening was the supermarket—something for supper—
and some long hours in her little flat where she knew
she would only brood, sifting over the events of last year
and asking herself if anything could have been different.

Susie was working evenings this week, and she had
too few other close friends here in Camberton now. One
had left to start married life in Scotland and another,
although friendly on the surface, was too patently critical,
underneath, about the way she had gone off with Paul.

Karen felt as if she had been cast adrift after a storm, and had to struggle against tears.

Then suddenly as she walked towards the bus-stop there was a white car, pulling up beside her, and she turned and, through her swimming eyes, saw Lee Shadwell at the wheel.

'I'll give you a lift,' he told her casually through the open driver's side window.

She was immediately appalled. To have this man. . . her boss. . .see her like this? No, thank you!

'It's all right,' she managed. 'The bus will be along soon.'

'Hmm.' A dismissive sound. He studied her in silence, the car's engine still idling quietly, and she knew that her colour was rising. As if she needed that—with eyes already noticeably pink, she was certain.

'I've. . .I've got something in my eye,' she told him feebly, though he hadn't commented on her state.

Why did she feel this compulsion to explain herself, as if that gold-flecked gaze of his were subjecting her to an inquisition? She turned away from him and dabbed the betraying wetness from her eyes with a tissue, before putting on a manufactured smile to insist, 'Really! Thanks for offering, but the bus. . .'

'I don't want to hear another word about the bloody bus!' he cut in, leaning across to open the passenger door with an authority that would not be denied.

'A lift would be nice,' she admitted, swept by a sudden wave of fatigue.

Just fatigue? Gropingly she realised that there was something about Lee, something. . .*nourishing*? Like the taste of good bread, fresh and warm from the oven, after a long diet of artificially flavoured sweets.

The low bucket seat of his car sighed and gave against her thighs with a welcoming pressure.

Watching her slide in beside him, Lee thought, I was

right to push it. She looks totally wrung out. Aloud, he said only, 'Can you manage the seat belt? It's stiff sometimes.'

'I—I think so.'

But she couldn't. It wouldn't click into place so, after a minute of watching her fumble with it, he reached across to help her and came into contact with fingers which had a clammy chill to them, although it wasn't yet all that cool outside.

She's really been through the mill, he thought again. A relative in hospital?

But, no, he didn't think she had any family in Camberton. If so, she had never mentioned them. Then he remembered the conversation that he couldn't help hearing at lunchtime today. The rude, impatient Paul and her shocked exclamation to him, 'In hospital? Where?'

He drove off, silent for some moments—as was she. But he couldn't help wondering; couldn't help his awareness of her. She had intrigued him from the beginning and he focused on this fact more deliberately now than he had allowed himself to do before, analysing his response.

Her looks, of course, were a part of it. That blonde, English-rose prettiness, warm and peachy. Those enticingly full curves, lovingly distributed over her rather small frame. She probably considered herself a little too plump, but Lee had a very male certainty that he would find those curves delicious beneath his hands.

Yes, he had to admit that his attraction to her was growing, and if his first response had been typically male and very physical there was more to it these days. For a start she was an excellent nurse and in his position he had to value that.

Sadly, there were some people who still washed up in nursing homes or similar facilities to Linwood because they saw it as a soft option, or because they couldn't compete in more technically demanding areas such as

Theatre or Intensive Care. They had no rapport with those who were chronically impaired, and sometimes didn't even try. But Karen Graham was one of an increasing number who weren't like that. She cared and she worked, and it showed.

But that wasn't the whole of it, either, he was beginning to realise. Glancing across at her as he turned out of the hospital driveway, he saw that she was still turned away from him—not realising how much her body language gave away her mood. This 'Paul' she had been visiting. . . He wasn't just some cousin with appendicitis. She wouldn't be so upset over something like that. It was more complex than wholehearted concern over someone who was ill.

Lee had sensed before that there was a surprising depth and complexity to Karen Graham's emotions. At twenty-eight she looked like someone who had had a happy and perhaps rather innocent and well-protected life but, from stray comments she had let slip and from her tolerance of even their least likeable patients, he guessed that she must know a little more of the dark side of life than first impressions would suggest.

He remembered something she had said a few weeks ago about Harry Makepeace, one of their regular day patients, confined to a wheelchair after a drunk-driving accident and very limited in what he could do for himself. His intermittent, but at times severe, alcohol abuse had made his family's lives miserable for years, but Karen's comment was surprisingly even-handed.

'Very few people are wholly evil, it seems to me, or wholly reprehensible. Harry isn't. I see no point in hating him for what he's done in his life. That's not going to help his wife, or his children. Let me find something about Harry to respect, and I'll do better in nursing him. That's my job.'

Lee found himself wondering what had given her this

outlook—wondering a lot of things about her—and before he had the chance to second-guess himself—first impulses were often the best ones, after all—he said easily, 'Doing anything tonight?'

'Pardon?' Yes, he had known she was miles away. 'Oh, tonight?' She looked in his direction for the first time, and he saw that her eyes were still red-rimmed. She struggled to find some humour. 'A *major* evening, actually. Single-handedly keeping Safeways from bankruptcy, then making a careful study of late twentieth-century culture as conveyed by the electronic media.'

'In other words, grocery shopping and the telly?' he drawled.

'Exactly!'

'Could you consider an exploratory epicurean expedition in conjunction with one-to-one verbal interface instead?'

She computed this rapidly, then laughed. 'Dinner with you. . .'

'Isn't that what I just said?'

They had stopped at a traffic light and he could see her watching him and weighing her next words, which came while the light was still red. 'Lee, I. . . It sounds very tempting, but I may not be the best company tonight. I've had a bit of a blast from the past just now, and it wasn't easy.'

Her honesty, though clearly reluctant, seemed to demand the same from him, and he returned calmly, 'I guessed as much. Surely that's a good reason for getting out and doing something else instead of brooding alone at home?'

'Perhaps, but why should you be the one to put up with me?'

'Because I owe you half an egg and lettuce sandwich?' he suggested lightly.

Her golden laugh came again, and he knew a satisfaction at the thought that he was doing something to alter her mood and make her forget that 'blast from the past'. *Paul?* For no very good reason, since he couldn't know for certain that the man on the phone was responsible for Karen's miserable mood, his deepest instinct was to detest him.

Then he realised, with a twinge of wry self-mockery, I'm jealous, that's what it is. Whoever he is, he has the power to make her *feel* and I don't—yet. Just the power to make her laugh.

Which was a start, he reflected, and he'd always believed in the power of small beginnings.

'All right,' she was saying, 'but. . .did you mean *out*? I'm. . .' she glanced down at the uniform she still wore beneath her light coat '. . .nothing but a dumpy little nurse in this.'

Actually, it contrasts perfectly with your golden blonde hair, and brings out the colour of your eyes and moulds across your breasts so that I have to drag my eyes away, but. . .'We can make it my place, if you'd like that better,' he suggested.

She hesitated for a second, then said, 'I would, I think.' She added quickly, 'Not that I'll stay late. . .'

'You certainly won't, Sister Graham, with a seven a.m. start tomorrow,' he returned, understanding that she needed some pledge of his honourable intentions. 'I'll deliver you home no later than ten.'

'Thanks. I— You're right, I think, Lee. I didn't want to go home alone. I'm really grateful for this.'

She trusts me. Good. And she won't have any reason to change her opinion on that point. 'Don't say that until you've sampled my beans on toast,' he warned her drily.

And she laughed again.

It took just three minutes for Karen to start regretting

her capitulation to Lee. Obviously she hadn't managed to hide from him that she was upset, and now she would have to spend the entire evening playing it down. If he offered her a shoulder to cry on and she had to fend it off, she had only herself to blame.

And if he thought she needed a lecture on keeping personal problems separate from the sphere of work... well, she agreed with that concept completely. In neither circumstance, though, did she want to give anything away, and yet it all burned inside her, unresolved, and to talk to someone...anyone but Lee...would be a mighty temptation.

They stopped at an Indian take-away and she had to forget her turmoil and consider the menu, a welcome distraction. Both of them expressed a preference for one heavily spiced dish, in contrast to a couple of others that were more fragrant on the palate, and then, with the hot bag of food steaming up the car windows, they drove for ten minutes more until they had left Camberton proper.

This was one of the hills behind the modest-sized city, where sheep-farming was beginning to give way to generous and well-planned subdivisions. Lee's house, in May light that was still bright and golden, was one of the original farmhouses, old and low and solid—not large—and made of sturdy Yorkshire stone. It was tucked into a hillside and overlooked a snaking railway line at the bottom of the valley, a village beyond and glimpses of Camberton beyond that.

It looked cosy and comfortable, inviting and warm. Inside she had the same impression from the solid but well-worn furniture, the motley assortment of well-loved knick-knacks and the collection of old raincoats and sou'westers hung on pegs behind the door and matched by military ranks of paired wellington boots. She couldn't help wondering how he came to live in a place like this.

It was none of her concern, of course, but it made her

realise—not for the first time—that there was a lot she didn't know about Lee Shadwell.

He took the bag of plastic food containers into the big farm kitchen and she started to follow him until he called back to her. 'Is the light blinking on my answering machine? It's on the telephone table—there by the fireplace.'

She found it, a slight anachronism in this old-fashioned place, and told him, 'Yes, it is.'

'How many blinks?'

'Oh...um, I mean, it's just blinking.'

'No, if you look, there's a pause and then you count the blinks and that's how many messages.'

'OK...' Although she was still sceptical she waited, watching the red light for a few seconds, and found that he was right. There was a pause then one, two, three... 'Eleven,' she told him. It seemed an unlikely number.

But he accepted it casually, then grinned. 'I'm not ringing them back. In fact, I'm not even listening to the tape.'

'Shame on you!' she teased. 'To leave all your girl-friends hanging by the phone all night!'

He grinned again, a distinctly wicked expression which pleated the skin around his eyes and turned his well-shaped mouth upside down at the corners. 'Is that what you think?'

'I could come up with some other theories, but it seems the most plausible,' she said. 'You're obviously used to it, or you'd be too curious to let that tantalising light blink all evening. *I* would be! *Eleven* phone calls! Which suggests that you're sure the calls are unimportant. Which somehow implies that the callers are. Which leads me to suspect a long string of frustrated and neglected girl-friends, who are all madly jealous of each other.'

'Oops, my secret's out,' he sighed. He was getting out plates and forks and serving spoons, and opening a bottle of white wine. 'And from your cynical tone I'd say there's no hope of persuading you to join their number.'

'None whatsoever,' she answered him, still speaking lightly.

Inside, though, she was thinking, He means just the opposite, of course. He probably has one very lovely girlfriend, and the only reason he asked me here was because he knew she'd be working late and wouldn't mind. Nice to have that level of trust! I let Paul destroy so much, including that. How do I get it back? I've been burnt and I can't return to how I used to be. . . . I'm not an innocent romantic any more. . .

She said aloud, to cut off the negative train of thought, 'Seriously, though, don't ignore the messages out of politeness.'

'I'm not,' he told her, coming through to put a soft classical CD into the player by the fireplace. 'I'm ignoring them because I know what they'll be about, and I can't face it all tonight.' She must have looked a little alarmed because he explained, 'Nothing serious. You see, I've somehow got myself on to two different committees this year, and there's always administrative business coming up. But if that light's driving you mad, blinking like that, I'll listen to them before we eat.'

'No, it's fine, really,' she told him quickly.

He unpacked the containers of food onto the kitchen table, along with the wine and glasses, plates and cutlery. They sat down and he took the lids off the containers and poured the wine while Karen watched, feeling an odd contentment rising in her now—just as the pale liquid rose in the tall-stemmed glasses.

The house was warm and tranquil and as homey as the old Victorian villa on the other side of Camberton where she'd spent a number of happy childhood years before her father's transfer to London. The music was sweet and soothing, and the steaming food fragrant and aromatically savoury. Since Lee saw her in the blue sister's uniform all day it didn't seem to matter that she was still wearing it now, in spite of his own well-fitting dark pants and white shirt—loosened at the neck now to show the masculine column of his throat.

It was so nice to feel that this was an unthreatening relationship with a man after Paul who, from the very beginning, had played on her so deliberately. Who had played on her illusions of romance, her ripe but untutored sensuality and her need to care and give—so that her response to the good-looking older man now seemed to her as involuntary and inevitable as a knee reflex.

In the spirit of this new friendship, she asked as they began to eat, 'Committees, Lee? What sort of committees?'

'Various youth organisations,' he explained. 'Fund-raising co-ordinator of one and secretary of another. Then there's a third. . . They want me to stand for treasurer at the coming annual general meeting, but I'm going to resist. Too much administration, and not enough grass-roots stuff. I like to help the kids—I like to enjoy myself—but at the moment it's mostly adding up budget figures and printing off newsletters.'

'You must be committed.'

'I *should* be committed, you mean,' he returned. 'Permanently! To a psychiatric institution. This latest project for the Camberton Youth Arts League is wildly over-ambitious, and it was all my idea.'

'I begin to understand why you're avoiding your phone messages.'

'Don't remind me,' he grinned. 'Perhaps you could ring everyone for me and tell them I've absconded with all the funds and emigrated to Argentina to buy up a few cattle ranches.'

'Cattle ranches?'

'Sounds more restful to me at the moment than my

current life.' It was obvious, however, that beneath these exaggerated complaints he relished the work he did in his spare time.

'Why did you go into nursing?' she asked on impulse, watching the neat, economical way he forked rice and fragrant chicken into his well-drawn mouth.

'I started getting interested in the caring professions in my teens,' he said, suddenly far more serious. 'My parents leased the land around this house for farming until it was resumed for the new subdivisions, but they were killed in a smash when I was seventeen and my younger brother was twelve.'

'Oh, Lee. . .'

'Yes, it was hard.' He nodded briefly. 'We were all close.' There was a tiny pause and Karen held her breath, not wanting to probe for more than he was prepared to reveal. He went on, 'We were split up and sent to different relatives who didn't know how to deal with us, and he had a nightmare of an adolescence. I managed to rescue him in the end, but— Look, it's a long story. . .'

'Don't tell it, then,' she came in, afraid that she had angered him and aware of her own need to be circumspect about the past. 'It was meant to be a simple question.'

'I know.' He grimaced attractively. 'You didn't know what you were letting yourself in for. Sorry.'

'No, I— It's—'

'Anyway, I think a deeply emotional experience at a crucial time in someone's development often leads to a need to *do* something. For other people? For the world? That's how it started for me. I didn't want to sell the house; there wasn't a lot of money aside from that, and my brother took a lot of commitment. I couldn't afford— financially or emotionally—too many years of demanding training. And nursing has a lot of scope—so many different career paths.

'I must say I didn't predict I'd end up at a place like

Linwood; into management and almost out of hands-on nursing—although I fight that. But it's a very satisfying career for me now, and I like the fact that it leaves me with the time and energy for other things.'

'Like too many committees?'

'Like too many committees,' he agreed ruefully.

There was a silence. Karen was thinking that being too busy sounded like an attractive idea at the moment. Not so much time to think. Or feel. . .

Paul.

She felt again that bewildering mixture of anger—at both him and herself—regret that she had ever let it happen at all and, in spite of it all, care. Yes, at some level, she still cared for him. How could she not? He had his virtues and his vulnerabilities like anyone else. Like old Harry Makepeace, for example, whom no one else could stand.

And Paul was so alone in the world. Like Lee's parents, Paul's were both dead but he hadn't been close to them and, for some strange reason that he had never succeeded in explaining to her, Paul and his elder brother had not been on speaking terms for nearly twenty years.

Not on speaking terms. Alone in the world. Just as she was now because of the way her mother had reacted to Paul during that horrible scene last October. She felt her mouth set into a pained, stubborn line, and the hurt threatened to overwhelm her again. This silence between herself and Lee had gone on for too long!

So she said quickly and over-brightly, 'Mmm! This curry *is* good!' and forked in the last untidy mouthfuls from her plate.

But he must have noticed her darkened mood. 'You had a difficult time up at the hospital today,' he suggested quietly. 'Do you want to talk about it?'

'No!' She shook her head vehemently at once. But to dramatise her reticence like that was as dangerous as spilling the whole story. She amended in a more even tone, 'I mean, there's not a lot to say. I was visiting. . . a friend.'

'Right. . .' His brown eyes saw too much.

'He's seriously ill,' she explained, compelled to by some quality in this man which she could not yet name. 'And he wanted me to see him. I'm worried about him, of course. But, please, let's not talk about it. I have no desire to—' Bore you. Burden you. Earn your distaste.

'Of course. Finish your meal,' he told her, and when she shook her head he proffered the curry containers more insistently. 'Come on! Can't have my staff getting themselves run down. Nursing is hard work.'

'You're right, of course,' she managed and helped herself, with a pretence of enthusiasm, to another serving.

The phone rang. They looked at each other and laughed. After those eleven phone messages. . .

'Is this going to be number twelve?' she asked.

'No,' he replied with a gusty sigh, 'because I'm going to do an incredibly heroic thing.'

'What's that?'

'I'm going to answer it.' He loped from the room and dived onto the instrument a fraction of a second before the end of the fifth ring, when the answering machine would have clicked on. 'Yup?' The casual bark of greeting was replaced almost at once by a more formal tone. 'Yes, this is Lee Shadwell. . . Yes, Sister Carter?'

There was no one on the staff at Linwood with that name. Karen began to work at her second helping—and it *was* work because the day's difficulties had left her with little appetite for a large meal—while she tried not to listen. A minute later, though, Lee was appealing for her help.

'It's Coronary Care at the hospital. . .'

'Not Mr Standish?' She stood up instinctively. He was such a delightful man. Surely. . .

'He's fine. At least,' Lee amended, with his hand covering the mouthpiece, 'physically fine. He's very distressed, apparently. That envelope I gave you that he wanted put somewhere safe. . .'

'Oh, yes.' She had to think for several seconds. 'On your desk. On a pile of— No, in a file tray, I think. Um. . .it was a bit of a mess.'

'The envelope?'

'Your desk!'

He grimaced guiltily. 'I know. One of my failings. But, then, I'd be maddening if I were perfect, wouldn't I?'

She choked.

'Seriously, though. . . He's asking for it, apparently; wants it brought to him; won't say what it is. Confidential. They've tried to fob him off; didn't want to bother me, but—'

'If you're going. . .'

'I must. If you don't mind.'

'Of course I don't. I'll come too.'

'There's no need.'

'Well, I hesitate to say this but, with the traffic in and out of your office this afternoon, you may never find that envelope without my help. In fact. . . Should I have put it in the safe? If it's got caught up with other papers. . .'

But it hadn't, much to their relief, and Karen located it easily enough in Lee's crammed in-tray.

'I can drop you home now,' he offered, but she shook her head.

'Let me come with you. I'm fond of Mr Standish, and I hate to think what might be bothering him. What's in that envelope, I wonder?'

'Something valuable—like savings bonds?' Lee suggested.

'Or a written confession of some dire deed in his past? You see the way my mind is working? If he's got something terrible on his mind. . .'

Mr Standish did. He looked grey and ill as they caught sight of him at the far end of a six-bed room in the coronary care unit at Camberton Hospital. Increasingly frail since his wife's death, he seemed to enjoy his regular attendance at Linwood's day hospital but had refused home help and the Linwood staff weren't convinced that he was looking after himself quite as well as he should.

Now he was staring into the distance, plucking at his sheet with an agitation that threatened to dislodge the IV line taped to his blue-veined hand, and Karen was glad that she'd persuaded Lee to let her remain involved tonight.

The elderly man's expression became urgent as soon as he saw them.

'You've got here in time,' he gasped, and his voice trembled. 'Thank goodness! Did you bring it? I—I don't think I've got the strength to write it all out again.'

'Yes, we brought it, Mr Standish,' Lee soothed, 'but please don't upset yourself like this.'

Mr Standish ignored the plea. 'Give it to me quickly so I can finish it. And you must stay and witness it, then take it to my solicitor in the morning. I'll give you his name and—'

'Whoa! Hang on a minute Mr Standish,' Lee came in, not quite managing to mask his alarm. 'What are we talking about here?'

'Why, my will, of course.'

'Your will?'

'Oh, don't waste my time, young man! I'm dying, and I must leave a valid will before I go or—'

'Who on earth told you you were dying?'

'I didn't need to be told,' he protested.

He was very tired, Karen could see, anxiety preventing him from getting the rest he needed. She looked at his drip and saw that it had stopped flowing, then ran a practised eye along the tubing and found a kink caused by his agitated movements. She straightened it unobtrusively, and the regular, silent rhythm of saline fluid dripping from the suspended bag commenced again.

Where were the staff? she wondered. Short-handed and therefore run off their feet, no doubt. She and Lee had been given a very cursory inspection when they entered the unit, and there was bustle and noise and light at the far end of the corridor, suggesting a crisis.

'I didn't need to be *told*!' Mr Standish repeated, fretful and shaky. 'They took one look at me and started putting in tubes and needles, and that heart specialist fellow didn't smile once when he was poking at me—just spouted a lot of medical gobbledygook so I wouldn't be able to understand.

'The nurses have been avoiding me, too, and I know what *that* means! They're scared of having to tell me. I suspected I wasn't long for this earth this afternoon when that pain wouldn't go so I started my will, but I didn't get a chance to finish. Tomorrow, I thought. That's why I left it with you but, then, tonight. . . What if I don't make it till morning? My hand's all shaky; I won't be able to write. . .' It was almost a moan as he flung his head back weakly onto the pillows.

'Please, Mr Standish!' Lee bent towards the bed and Karen took the old man's trembling hand. 'Listen to me, will you, old mate? I sincerely doubt that you're dying. You've got a drip and a catheter. I expect your fluids were a bit low, that's all. Did they tell you to drink a lot?'

'They did give me a jug of water. . .'

'Look, I'm going to check your notes.'

The folder was in a rack at the foot of the bed and he flipped it open and studied it quickly, raising his head a few minutes later to say, 'Yes, it's as I thought. Your blood pressure was a bit low and your temperature was slightly up, suggesting some mild dehydration. Mr

Elliott, the consultant cardiologist, took a look at you, apparently, and has scheduled you for a test or two tomorrow. Now, for a start, I've run across that man several times and I've never once seen him crack a smile, so that *wasn't* his pre-funeral face that you saw.

'And, secondly, he's already noted down a likely diagnosis for your heart problem, and it's something very minor in one of your valves which can be controlled with a different medicine.'

There was silence for quite some time as Fred Standish absorbed all this, and Karen held her breath as her glance locked fleetingly with Lee's to read her own concern mirrored there.

Mr Standish grimaced, rubbed his eyes with his free hand, then looked at them and said squarely, 'Well, I'm a silly old fool, then, aren't I?' He gave a bark of laughter. 'Wasting your time; getting you both up here in the middle of the night.'

'Hardly that, Mr Standish,' Karen assured him. 'It's only nine o'clock.'

'Seems like the middle of the night—the way they feed you and turn down the lights so early,' he retorted.

He was a completely new man, his colour returning and the aura of frailty markedly diminished as he pulled himself up higher in the bed. 'A bit low in fluids, and a minor valve problem,' he crowed after a moment. 'Well, well. And me worrying over my will, as if I had millions to leave and half a dozen children to disinherit.' There was an ironic chuckle. 'You'll be rolling your eyes, both of you, the moment you're out of this door, won't you?'

'Not at all,' Karen said. 'We're glad to have sorted it out for you, aren't we, Lee? If you hadn't sent for that will of yours you might have worried about this all night.'

'Nice young people,' Mr Standish said. 'Get along with you now, then, and don't let me jaw at you all night.'

'Are you sure you're all right, Mr Standish?' Lee said.

'Better than I've been since Eunice died,' he answered. 'She always told me I had years left in me and I should enjoy them, but I never took her seriously. Now I think perhaps I will!'

He looked so zesty that it appeared he might leap out of bed then and there, and Lee was constrained to warn him, 'Get a good night's rest for now, and start enjoying life tomorrow — OK, Mr Standish?'

'Now that's good sense, yes. This bed feels a darn sight more comfortable than it did a few minutes ago!' He muttered once more, 'Low blood pressure and slight fever, indeed!'

They left him, with full colour in his cheeks now and the once-precious envelope containing his half-finished will sitting disregarded on the night-table. In the corridor, a moment later, Lee said to Karen, 'That's the sort of mood-elevator I wish we could bottle and dispense by the spoonful!'

'Isn't it just?' she agreed. 'But if I was running this ward I'd have a stern talk to whichever nurses *didn't* explain to him exactly what was going on and interpret the great Mr Elliott's wisdom into plain language for him.'

'Don't worry,' Lee said. 'I'm *not* running this ward, but I intend to talk sternly to someone about it anyway.' He glanced along the corridor as they reached the lift. 'Not now. They're obviously in the middle of a resuscitation.'

They heard a doctor's urgent shout, 'OK, shock him again. Another fifteen seconds, and get those drugs into him.'

'I'll ring Coronary Care tomorrow, talk to someone about what happened and get the official word on Mr Standish's condition as well.'

'It's our fault, too,' Karen realised aloud. '*My* fault, I suppose. And my excuse is the same as it undoubtedly is here. Too busy. We sent him off in the ambulance in between handling ten other jobs, and didn't make sure he understood that this chest pain could mean any number of things that weren't life-threatening.'

'Don't kick yourself. It was what they did to him here that got him alarmed, not the pain itself,' Lee said. 'Come on, now. This hasn't been quite the evening I promised you, and I want to drop you home.'

'It's been a very nice evening, actually,' Karen told him sincerely, comparing it inwardly with the one she would have spent at home.

They entered the lift, and when it stopped at the floor where the chest ward was located she couldn't help an irrational trepidation as the doors opened. . . But the older nurse who entered was no one she knew—no one connected with Paul.

And, if she had been, why would it have mattered? Karen was forced to ask of herself. The answer to the question—the very *human* answer—shifted on his feet as they neared the ground floor, bringing his warmth within reach of her senses. Oddly, this made her shiver and become aware that she was a little chilly herself.

Lee noticed her convulsive movement, slight though it was. 'Cold?'

'Just a bit.' She was disturbed at his perception. If he was as sensitive to her moods as he was to her physical state. . .

I mustn't let Paul make a difference to my focus at work because Lee *would* notice, and I couldn't bear that—to jeopardise my job. . .

She couldn't help being too silent in the car as they drove from the hospital to her small flat. She'd told Lee the address, and he knew the street so she couldn't even paper over the silence with giving directions.

At the wheel, Lee felt her mood like something physical. A fog. . .or a third entity, making an unwanted presence in the car. A malign ghost, perhaps. . .or another man. The one she had talked about—or more accurately, had *not* talked about—over dinner. The one who was in hospital.

Lee instinctively mistrusted the man and the set-up, even while recognising that he knew nothing about either. But he had a certain emotional antenna when it came to human problems—perhaps that was why he'd been drawn to nursing—and he *knew*. . . What? That she was distressed about more than just this man's health.

Which somehow drew out the attraction to her that he hadn't fully acknowledged until today and made it far more urgent so that, when they stopped outside her flat after several minutes of silent driving, he obeyed his primal male impulse and turned her into his arms.

The kiss was feather-light, a quest—tightly reined in—for her response. She tasted as good as he had known she would. Better. And, although she had stiffened and gasped at his first movement towards her, she had not pulled her mouth away from the touch of his lips.

His lips. . . Such a butterfly pressure, such a fleeting moment of sweetness that it seemed to be over before Karen fully understood that it had happened, and her overwhelming sensation was one of need—need for it to go on. She hadn't expected his kiss at all; had already been preparing some rather stiff little words of thanks and goodnight. He was her boss, after all. Hadn't she just concluded that that was why she must keep Paul and her regrets and questions so completely to one side?

And now this, and her unexpected reaction to it. Startled, her eyes met his gold-flecked regard and he must have seen something in her face—something that she didn't yet fully recognise herself—because his eyes were close enough for her to drown in now, his mouth was closing over hers once more and this time his kiss wasn't feather-light and fleeting at all.

Yet it was tender, as if he was exploring the sensation of it. His tongue touched the inner corner of her mouth and then he nibbled with tantalising softness at her full lower lip, making her mouth open to receive and taste him. His cheek was a little roughened now by the day's growth of beard, and in the tiny moments when his lips left hers his breath was a hot, rhythmic fan.

Karen crumbled inside, a melting mass of sensation so unexpected that her own breathing became a series of rapid, uneven pants. The thought that she might be attracted to Lee was utterly new, yet it felt, in this moment, unexpectedly right. His arms were fully around her now, warm and hard and male—as was the chest that pressed against her breasts, grazing them into tingling life.

But it was this deeper arousal that told her abruptly that their kiss should end. There was something frightening about it—about the sudden strength of her response—and she needed time to think. She had never given herself that luxury with Paul, to her bitter regret, and that headlong, star-struck plunge was something she had vowed never to repeat.

All this she knew only very hazily as Lee's kiss continued to swamp her senses. Opening her eyes—she didn't remember closing them—she saw the dark, satiny fan of lashes against his cheeks and was disturbed to see that he was as lost in this as she was.

'Lee?'

His warm, fathomless eyes drifted open, and he murmured against her mouth, 'Knew it would feel this good. Did you?'

'N-no, I didn't.' She blurted the confession. It emerged as a husky whisper, sensual, which she hadn't intended at all. 'I never thought about it until. . .well, until it happened.'

'No. . .?'

'And now it's. . . I'm sorry, I—'

'You have absolutely no need to be sorry about any-thing,' he told her, authoritative and gentle at the same time.

'No, but I—I don't want to set up expectations.'

'Listen, you haven't promised to ransom me your first-born. We kissed. And it was nice. That's all. We'll take it from there. Or *not*, as the case may be. OK?'

'OK,' she nodded.

He had released her a little, and now his hands were enclosing hers—so warm. . . She shivered uncontrollably once more, and he smiled. 'You really are cold, aren't you?'

'N-not where it counts,' she answered confusedly, staring at their joined hands so that she missed the brief flare of satisfaction in his gaze.

'Better go in,' he said several moments later, and only then did she realise that she must have been staring like that without moving for far too long.

'Y-yes.'

'I'll wait till your light comes on inside. See you tomorrow.'

'Thanks,' she managed and opened the door, shocked at her reaction. He was the one who had initiated that disturbingly powerful kiss, yet it was she who now seemed most under its thrall.

Hurrying through the front door of her very nonde-script building, she touched her tongue to her lower lip—as if licking away a grain of rice—and almost thought that she could still taste him there.

Why am I making so much of it? she scolded herself. As Lee says, it was just a kiss. . . Only I wasn't even ready for that. After Paul. . . Then she smiled as she remembered Lee's own perspective. But no, I haven't promised him my first-born. Trust him to put it like that!

Oddly warmed inside, she breasted the top of the stairs,

put her key in the lock and flooded her tiny flat with light. Outside Lee hooted once and she quickly went to wave from the window, then saw him drive away into the night.

CHAPTER THREE

BREAKFAST at Linwood was an important meal, and a busy one. This was a fact that the newly arriving day staff could be heard to lament on occasion. Today Karen cautiously admitted to herself that she was glad of the chance to plunge into the mêlée immediately after the end of the seven a.m. shift-change report. Lee sometimes made an appearance at report but he hadn't this morning—another cause for relief.

This way, when I do see him, I'll be too busy to do more than say hi.

It was silly to be planning the moment—like planning a battle strategy—but she couldn't help it. Overnight, 'just a kiss' had stayed with her far more than she had wanted it to. It had coloured her dreams, distracted her senses, robbed her of her appetite and almost made her late for work, and now. . .

'Pete, do you want to sit next to Charlotte again this morning?'

She faced the sixteen-year-old boy in order to read the reply he signalled with a movement of his eyes—upwards for 'yes'. She wasn't surprised. He'd been here a week now, and he and seventeen-year-old Charlotte gravitated towards each other whenever they could. Unfortunately Charlotte's two weeks of respite care would end tomorrow and she would go home.

'Have you two exchanged phone numbers yet?' she asked him impulsively. Pete was new to Camberton and was not yet hooked in to the various support and social networks in the area, but his cerebral palsy was of a similar degree of severity to Charlotte Hampton's. If their friendship could continue. . .

But this time he gave a half-blink to mean 'no', and looked rather downcast.

'Waiting for her to make the first move, eh?'

Talk about making a move! Karen jumped visibly at the sound of Lee's voice. Lee had been close enough to have read Pete Larkins's expression and yet she hadn't heard his approach at all, masked as it had been by the squeak and thud of wheelchairs and walking-frames, the crash of trays and crockery and the ocean-like swell of conversation.

Pete cracked up. He had a ready sense of humour. During his first year of life his appropriately timed laughter had been one of the first clues to his loving and supportive parents that his intelligence was normal, and subsequent tests had proved it to be well above average. At the moment it wasn't clear whether he was laughing at Lee's question or Karen's electric response.

It was the latter, according to Lee. 'Quite a reaction! Got a guilty conscience?' He drawled the suggestion to her in an aside that Pete wouldn't hear.

It was too close to the truth. . .and Lee was too close to *her*! She felt his warmth graze her bare arm and was enveloped in the male aura of his scent, which was as fresh as newly blanched almonds.

She made light of her betraying reaction. 'A guilty conscience? Sure have! With four phone calls, three sets of case notes, two discharge reports—'

'And a partridge in a pear tree?'

'—that I haven't got done yet, so if you'll excuse me. . .'

'With pleasure, since you've just wheeled Pete's chair onto my foot.' He brushed her waist lightly with a caressing hand, and she was girdled in tingling sensation.

Pete cracked up again at Lee's words.

'Lee, don't,' Karen appealed, flicking her gaze to meet his so that he could easily read how flustered she was.

He was smiling, just a little, as he murmured something that she didn't quite catch about 'small beginnings'. And Pete's chair wheel *was* on his foot. She wheeled the teenager quickly to the far side of the large dining-room, where Charlotte followed his approach with every bit of the pleasure she felt visible in her dark eyes. When you had severe cerebral palsy and could only communicate with your eyes those 'windows to the soul' couldn't afford to beat about the bush.

Karen's own gaze had just expressed her confused, complex feelings to Lee—*about* Lee—almost as frankly.

This time yesterday I knew I liked him but I had no idea I was attracted to him—yet I am, and he knows it, and he's pleased, and—

I'm terrified.

She didn't need this now! Not with Paul Chambers back in Camberton. Sitting down between Pete and Charlotte to help them eat, as both had too little arm and hand control to manage self-feeding, she had to drag her thoughts back to the present and wasn't fully successful. Charlotte gagged and lost the spoonful of cereal Karen had just given her.

'I'm sorry, Charlotte.' She bit her lip. This was no good! Both teenagers enjoyed their food and ate neatly, with the ability to chew and swallow normal meals as long as everything was finely cut, but they needed good co-ordination with whoever was helping—real team-work—and at the moment Karen knew that she wasn't concentrating as she should.

She was ashamed, especially when Charlotte turned her dark eyes expressively in Lee's direction and raised her eyebrows—her way of asking a question.

Karen nodded and said lightly, 'Yes, he was teasing me. Teasing Pete, too. Must confess I started that. But we're both wondering when you two are going to exchange phone numbers.'

Charlotte blushed and laughed but looked eager, and Pete was staring downwards. Karen recognised his reaction as shyness, not reluctance.

'Shall I fix it up with your parents, then?'

Since Pete and Charlotte could produce only a limited repertoire of sounds and used various written tools for greater communication—new computerised wordboards were a current and on-going experiment—there would have to be considerable parental help if this relationship was to progress beyond tomorrow. Fortunately both the Larkins and the Hamptons were sensible and highly motivated when it came to their children's welfare, and Karen was sure that things would go smoothly.

Things appeared to be going smoothly throughout the dining-room at the moment. Patients were still being wheeled in or, if mobile, helped to their seats, and some of the early arrivals were well into their meal. No breakfast in bed at Linwood!

There were usually several Alzheimer's patients in residence and they were often at their best at this time of day—more co-operative, more competent, more likely to be orientated in time and place and more able to recognise familiar people. For them, being up for breakfast made a sensible prelude to daily washing or bathing.

For much of the year most of the children in residence had school, and had to be ready to leave in good order. Additionally, the sense of community was increased when everyone was gathered together like this. Lee felt strongly that the different age or disability groups should mix together as much as possible, and Karen agreed with him.

His was an original approach in many areas. Today, for instance, he wore the uniform of a male nurse, a sign that this was to be one of his self-declared 'hands-on' days. It was his way of staying in touch with the day-to-day problems and concerns of the nursing staff, and meant that he could never be accused of having sold out to management.

'I *never* eat in my dressing-gown!' Karen heard the statement just behind her as she continued to feed Pete and Charlotte. It was Mrs Masterton, a very elegant and fastidious old lady, and Lee was wheeling her to her place at the next table.

His reply to her complaint was courteous. 'I know you're not the only one to feel that way, Mrs Masterton. But we have to get the school-kids off first thing, you see, and we can't manage to help everyone with dressing in time. You'd hate to be hurried, wouldn't you? Or to get a cold breakfast and stewed tea?'

'Oh, indeed! Indeed I would! No, you're right, of course. The children mustn't be late for their schools. If anyone else complains I'll let them know the establishment's policy.'

She was a funny old thing, Mrs Masterton—unfailingly fastidious in her grooming, rather stiff and occasionally very irritable. Since she was a fully paying patient, she seemed to take the attitude that respite care was a kind of hotel accommodation, and her frequently uttered statement that she 'lived alone, quite independently' would have drawn raised eyebrows from her hard-working daughter.

Lucy Stevens single-handedly managed laundry, shopping, cooking, cleaning and gardening for her mother in a big old house—several miles from her own place—which old Mrs Masterton refused to exchange for a smaller, more convenient dwelling. As she had only been living there for the past ten years, this stubbornness couldn't quite be excused on grounds of sentiment.

Mrs Stevens had gone away for two weeks to attend her own daughter's wedding in the United States and, after initially betraying real fear about her abandonment, Mrs Masterton now seemed genuinely convinced that the respite care stay had been entirely her own very felicitous idea.

This morning she treated Lee like a waiter at her favourite restaurant, calling him 'young man' and. . .*flirting* with him? Surely Karen's ears must be deceiving her there! But, as she met his gaze across the two tables that separated them and caught the wry humour in his brown eyes, her perception was confirmed.

'There certainly is something about a man in uniform,' Mrs Masterton pronounced.

'Is that what's getting to me today?' Karen muttered darkly to herself.

'The white suits you, young man. It really looks. . . almost *naval*. Were you ever in the senior service?'

'Mrs Tostell's daughter is very keen to have her continue as a day patient, in spite of the ankle injury,' Lee reported to Karen later. 'The question is can we handle it?'

'What do you think?' she countered, then could have kicked herself. Talk about feeble! She was alone with him, and it had happened a dozen times before, but all of a sudden she was going to pieces about it. Her heart was thudding when it should have been merely pumping in its usual quiet way, and his strong body was like a magnet—pulling her gaze.

'Well, she's under doctor's orders to keep all weight off the leg until it's X-rayed again in four weeks' time,' he was saying, as briskly as if they'd only just met. 'Effectively, that means we're exchanging a mobile, self-caring day patient—albeit a fairly demanding one, with some continence problems—for a wheelchair patient who'll need assistance with toileting and transport, and probably won't be too gracious about it. Since we've just taken on three more elderly wheelchair patients with poor prognosis for increased ambulation. . .'

Karen sighed, and succeeded in gathering her thoughts. 'Have we heard from the community staff?'

'Yes, they'd like her to keep coming. Although we see her as fairly crusty she's a lot worse if she's bored, apparently, and the daughter still has two teenagers at home, as well as a new grandson across the other side of town who she's dying to spend time with.'

'We can keep having her, as far as I'm concerned. It's such a slight injury, really.'

'I hate to see the nursing staff getting squeezed ever tighter,' Lee said. 'But ultimately I agree. To knock her back over something like this. . . I'll phone now and tell them the good news. Meanwhile, Dr Stone is due at any minute to listen to some chests.'

'That's right, I knew we had something special on this morning.'

'Here's the list. I suggest you have the first patient waiting for her in the treatment room and then just shuttle them back and forth continuously. By the time you've dropped off the previous patient and collected the next one, Dr Stone should have just about finished with the one she's actually seeing.'

'Sounds complicated.'

'It isn't, if you think about it,' he told her cheerfully. So she did, and found that he was right.

'And you'd like me to do it?'

'Yes, because this is something new we're trying here—having various specialists come in to evaluate certain patients, rather than sending them off individually to a clinic. I'd like to get your opinion afterwards on whether it works for staff and patients, and I'd like Dr Stone's opinion as well.'

So Karen took the list and collected the first patient on it from Tuesday morning sing-along. It happened to be Honoria Masterton, who had two lovely spots of colour on her cheeks and faded blue eyes that sparkled.

'Oh, I *do* enjoy singing the old songs!' she said as Karen took her arm and helped her down the corridor. 'Some people think it's silly, like nursery school, but I say nonsense! If we're too full of our own importance to have a bit of childish fun. . . And it takes one's mind off. . .off all the things that are not so nice.'

She frowned, her elation seeping away, and Karen wondered what the 'not so nice' things were that had clearly crowded back into Mrs Masterton's mind now. She said carefully, 'Yes, you can't be sad when you're singing in a group, can you? Even if it's a sad song.'

'No, you can't. Did you hear us doing "Lili Marlene"?'

'No, I came in for the last bit of "Green Grow the Rushes, Oh".'

'That song was such a wonderful mystery to me as a child. *It's* a bit sad, really. "One is one and all alone. . ."'

'". . .And evermore shall be so,"' Karen finished.

Mrs Masterton sighed. 'Well, here we are, then. Must soldier on regardless. Can't have people thinking we can't cope.' She seemed to be talking to herself.

Sitting down in the little waiting area outside the treatment room, she smoothed her dark maroon skirt neatly along her thighs with her thin, blue-veined hands. Her back was ramrod straight in the moulded plastic chair.

Megan Stone appeared in the doorway at that moment, black medical bag in hand and an immaculate white coat atop her light cashmere sweater and grey wool skirt. She said a friendly goodbye to Linwood's part-time physiotherapist, Gaye Wyman, with whom she had clearly been chatting as they walked along the corridor, then frowned at the sight of Karen.

'Oh! It's Karen Graham, isn't it?'

Karen flushed a little. 'Yes, I'm working here at Linwood now.'

The tall, beautiful chest specialist nodded slowly as Karen opened the treatment room door for her. A dedicated and caring doctor, Megan Stone could sometimes be downright intimidating to more junior staff, although Karen suspected that it wasn't intentional.

Beneath the aura of intelligence and ability there was a degree of very human warmth—self-doubt, perhaps, as well—and Karen had always thought that she would like Dr Stone if she met her in some non-threatening circumstance—both dressed in jeans, say, throwing balls to their dogs in the park.

Today, though. . .

'Hmm,' Dr Stone was saying thoughtfully. Then, with blunt directness, she said, 'Look, do you have some time after I finish here?'

'I— Probably, yes. I'll be due for lunch.'

'Because I'd like to talk to you about what's going on with Paul Chambers.'

Karen heard her own hissing in-breath but managed to control her face. 'Is. . .there a problem?'

'You came to see him yesterday, didn't you?'

'Yes.'

'He's not doing very well, and— Look, we can't talk now. I do hate to keep elderly patients waiting. Afterwards, all right?'

'Of course.'

'Thanks, Karen.' She smiled, and the beautiful face softened to reveal its warmth as well as its intelligence. 'Bring Mrs Masterton in now, would you?'

Dr Stone was seeing seven patients this morning and by the end of the little clinic Karen was having to collect them from the dining-room, where a hot lunch was already in progress. The session had gone smoothly, and three of the patients had said that it was 'much easier than having to go up to the hospital'.

Dr Stone seemed pleased too. 'Mostly, there's nothing

to add to the picture from their GPs or previous clinic visits. But there are two that I'd like to come up for an X-ray, and I'm going to change the medication that Mrs Masterton and Mr Langley are using. There's something newer out now which has fewer reported side-effects, and it's so often the side-effects that are such a curse in geriatric medicine.'

'I know,' Karen agreed. 'At times they can be harder on old bodies than the problem for which the drug was prescribed in the first place.'

'Which is why this sort of reassessment is important,' Dr Stone agreed. 'I hate to hear that someone's been chugging along with the same old drug at the same old dose for months—or even years—without a re-evaluation. . . I've written out the scripts. Should I give them to you?'

'Yes, thanks, and I'll pass Mrs Masterton's on to the pharmacy myself and give Mr Langley's to his daughter.'

'Keep an eye on them for a few days to make sure they really do do better with the new stuff,' Dr Stone advised. 'Now, our talk. . .I don't have a lot of time, unfortunately, as we went late. Is there some lunch I could get here?' It was said apologetically, but then her stomach rumbled and both women laughed.

'There's the patients' lunch,' Karen suggested sympathetically. The specialist's breakfast had obviously been eaten some hours ago. 'We usually don't find it all that appetising after helping all our patients to eat it so we bring our own, but it really is very nice.'

'But I'd like to talk to you privately. . .'

'The staff room,' Karen said. 'I'm on early break today, so there probably won't be anyone else there.'

'Sounds good. I wish I had more than twenty minutes. . .'

Karen fetched a bowl of soup and a vegetable pie from the kitchen and met up with Megan in the staff room several minutes later, sitting across the table from her with her own sandwiches—for which suddenly she had no appetite at all. Megan wanted to talk about Paul. . .

And she did, launching into the subject without any pretence at small talk—which was perhaps kinder in the long run.

'You were, um, living with him for a while, weren't you?'

'Yes, but it. . .didn't last.'

'You're no longer involved at all, then?'

'I— No. I visited him yesterday, as you've obviously heard, and I'm planning to bring him some books he's asked for, but it's out of—of friendship. . .' As she said the word it tasted totally wrong in her mouth. She and Paul weren't friends. Had never been friends. She went on quickly, 'Not out of. . .anything else.'

Dr Stone nodded slowly, then, testing her words said, 'I think he'd like you back.'

'Dr Stone—'

She went on quickly, 'Look, I admit I'm seeing this as a doctor. Nathan Fleischman is overseeing his case, but—'

'Nathan Fleischman?' The name was unfamiliar to her.

'Yes, that's right; you'd left by the time he came on board. A visiting fellow from Boston, where Nick Darnell is now working.'

'Of course, Dr Darnell went to Boston for a year.'

'Mmm.' Megan shifted uncomfortably, and Karen remembered the suspicion she had had last year that the lovely blonde doctor had rather a horrible crush on her attractive and very married forty-year-old senior. She didn't say anything about it now, of course.

'Anyway,' Megan went on quickly, 'we've strayed from the point, haven't we? This has nothing to do with the Darnells. As I started to say, Dr Fleischman is very worried about him—as am I. He's not responding to the drugs so far and his morale is very low, as you may have seen.'

'Yes, I—'

The doctor leaned forward, earnest and appealing—her rapidly cooling soup still untouched. 'Look, if there's really too much water under the bridge between the two of you then please ignore what I'm saying, but. . . Well, you did take a very big step in going off with him last year.'

'That's certainly true. . .'

'And if there's anything left—if this is just a lover's quarrel or, I don't know, some rift that can be bridged; please don't think I'm trying to pry into the details—couldn't you try to reconsider? Paul's lungs are quite badly damaged now, permanent damage which will remain even if we can rid him of the disease once and for all—and notice that I said "if"!'

'You mean you really are worried that he might not pull through?'

'The strain of TB he has is proving fatal in the United States in similar circumstances,' Megan said quietly. 'Dr Fleischman has seen it himself.'

'Don't do this to me, Dr Stone,' Karen said tightly. She was too upset to be anything but honest, and too upset to stay seated any longer. She began to roam the staff room, which she found far too small today. 'Don't make me responsible. It's what Paul did all the time. It's why, or part of why I— Oh, God!'

She hid her face in her hands and there was a cry of consternation from Megan.

'Oh, Karen, I'm not blaming you or trying to put his destiny in your hands. Please don't think that! I just wanted to say that if there was anything that could swing the balance for you then, perhaps, this should be it. But if it's impossible please disregard what I've said.'

'I'll think about it, Dr Stone,' Karen managed. 'I'll

think about everything you've brought up.'

The other woman was frowning over her untouched soup. 'Perhaps I shouldn't have—'

'No,' Karen assured her quickly, 'you did the right thing. I—I needed to know. I don't want to abandon him.'

'I'll leave you to think about it, then, as I *must* get back,' Megan said, rising to her feet. She waved at the soup apologetically. 'I'm afraid I haven't. . . But I'll take the pie.'

She left, still obviously concerned at the effect of what she had said, and Karen couldn't quite manage to suppress her own feelings. Mechanically, she washed the soup down the sink, having no appetite for it nor for her own sandwiches, then she pressed her face into her hands and groaned aloud—not registering Lee's voice in conversation with Dr Stone just out in the corridor until it was too late and he had entered.

'My God, what's wrong?' His voice cracked and she whirled around, dragging her hands from her face but knowing that her tightly pressed fingers must have left blotchy marks there against her fair skin.

'I'm all right, Lee.' She saw him as if through a barrier of fog, and it was suddenly *impossible* that he had kissed her last night. It wouldn't happen again. She didn't want it—couldn't *afford* it now—and he wouldn't want it if he knew. . .

'No, you're not all right!' He was correct, of course. 'It wasn't Dr Stone, was it? Giving you a dressing-down? If there was a problem this morning—'

'No, nothing like that. I like Dr Stone very much.' She dragged her mind back to her work and pumped a cheerful professionalism into her tone. 'It went well. The patients seemed to find it convenient, and Dr Stone found some things she wants followed up.'

She summarised the chest specialist's recommendations briefly, but Lee came in with crisp impatience almost before she had finished, 'Forget about all that for now. I'm glad it went well, but it can wait. What's upset you so badly?' Then he amended at once, 'No! I'm sorry. It's none of my business.'

'That's all right, Lee,' she answered him vaguely.

'Although I'm concerned, of course. I hate to see... my staff unhappy.'

'It won't affect my work,' she assured him—too fervently.

There had been accusations of that last year at the hospital and she knew that they weren't true, but rumours spread so easily in the world of health care... Would Megan Stone talk to Lee about Paul, for example? 'If anyone says anything, please give me the benefit of the doubt.'

Puzzlement and concern were etched into his features, which was hardly surprising. What she'd said didn't exactly add up to clarity or reassurance. He had no idea what she was talking about, and since she was still determined not to tell him...

'I'm sorry, Lee, I'm not making much sense.'

'No, you're not,' he agreed in a drawl. He looked wary, as if afraid that she might suddenly launch into complete hysteria, and on an impulse of which she was unconscious until it was too late she reached out and touched his arm.

'Can we forget all this...?' They both looked down at her fingers, curved over the bare skin of his forearm. It was hard and male and roughened by golden hairs and it felt so good beneath her hand that she quickly removed it and stepped away, to continue as firmly as she could, 'I do have some personal difficulties at the moment, as you've guessed, but I'll deal with them in my own time. I— Really, that's all I want to say.'

'Did I give the impression of wanting to probe?' he asked lightly.

'No, you didn't. I didn't mean to suggest that. It's me...being over-sensitive about the whole thing. So—can we forget it?'

'Of course, and, with that in mind, here's a distraction—something you're *not* to forget.' He stacked a small pile of leaflets on the table. 'The Youth Arts League's Medieval Fair on Saturday.'

'Oh, right!' The change of subject was as much of a relief to him as it was to her, she could see. 'The culprit behind your eleven phone messages?'

'Nine of them,' he agreed. 'Amazingly enough, one was actually from a friend.'

'And the other?' she teased, although the humour was still an effort. 'A wrong number?'

'The local library. I have overdue books,' he confessed.

'Which you wouldn't, if you weren't too busy with the Medieval Fair to have returned them?'

'Exactly. Do you think you might manage to come? There'll be jousting displays, archery, feasting, crafts. . . I'm going to pester the entire staff all week, so it would be best if you all capitulated immediately and promised to bring everyone you've ever met.'

'In that case. . .' It sounded fun. If Susie was off work that day they might go together. And it was obvious that Lee and his group deserved support for the venture. He fanned the leaflets out across the table so that no one could possibly miss them and then ducked out of the room, leaving her alone once more.

She decided suddenly, even if Susie can't make it, I'll go by myself. I have to start finding a real life here for myself once more. It's a long time since I've done anything so simply good fun as going to a fair.

Which decision brought her back to Paul again and Dr Stone's disturbing suggestion. She made a cup of tea and managed to eat her sandwiches, brooding over the whole thing—searching her conscience and her heart and her head, and ending up with nothing any clearer in her mind, it seemed. Other staff members began to arrive for their lunch-breaks and they all examined and discussed Lee's leaflets, then it was time for Karen to return to work. It came as a relief to be able to concentrate on the problems of others.

CHAPTER FOUR

THERE were two admissions to deal with first.

'It seems so typical that this hiking trip Steve and the boys have been planning for so long should come right in the middle of the most severe exacerbation I've had yet!' said Mary Thomas cheerfully as Karen sat down with her to go over all the admission details. 'And thank goodness you had a place for me here! I'd been hoping I could manage at home alone, with my sister coming in for a while each day, but with my body suddenly going on strike like this. . .'

Forty-seven-year-old Mrs Thomas had been diagnosed with multiple sclerosis twelve years earlier, when the younger of her two boys was only four years old, and the progress of her disease had been moderate since then. As with almost all MS sufferers, though, the inevitable worsening of her condition did not proceed steadily but came in the form of exacerbations which might last for several weeks, followed by lengthy remissions during which she felt and functioned far better once again.

Mary's case notes suggested that she was the kind of multiple sclerosis patient who inspired others to try harder—accepting of the reality of her disease, yet constantly fighting to find the best way of dealing with its many symptoms. Her current exacerbation had forced her into a wheelchair for the first time, and she admitted, 'There are a lot of tricks I still have to learn about this. That's the good thing about having to come here while the men are away. I'm hoping you'll have all sorts of tips for me!'

'We'll try,' Karen promised.

68

They finished going through all the admission details together, and Karen was left with a great deal of admiration and liking for this woman who managed to talk about even the worst of her symptoms in a cheerful and sensible way.

Her next admission was less easy to handle. They had been expecting Ross North yesterday but he hadn't turned up, and a phone call to his house late in the afternoon had elicited only a vague response. This morning, too, staff had been on the look-out for his arrival, but he hadn't come. There was no answer on the phone at the North residence.

Now, at last, here he was, a thirty-seven-year-old quadriplegic with hostility and resentment etched into every line of his rather handsome face. His wife was with him. She was a pretty, dark-haired woman and together they made an attractive couple, but she did not look happy either and the distance and tension between the pair were almost palpable.

After showing Mr North the room he would share with one other patient, Karen sat the couple down and began to go over his patient history and take down the same admission details she had obtained from Mary Thomas. But they had barely got as far as the diving accident which had broken his neck and almost completely severed the spinal cord two years ago when Mrs North cleared her throat and stood up hesitantly.

'I'll go, I think. My train leaves in two hours, and I still have to get the children to my sister's.'

'Going away?' Karen queried lightly.

'Just to Devon. For a week. I—need some time to myself.'

Ross North muttered something profane between clenched teeth, and Karen saw his wife's face set hard with a mixture of anger and pain.

'Bye, Ross,' she said briefly. She made a tiny movement towards him as if to kiss him, then changed her mind and moved briskly to the door. 'I'll phone.'

'Don't put yourself out,' he growled sourly.

Mrs North ignored this. 'Nice to meet you, Sister Graham.' A piece of perfunctory politeness. Her hands were clenched and every line of her figure tightened with tension.

'Enjoy your—' Karen began, but Jill North had gone.

There was a moment of very hostile silence from Mr North while Karen groped to get back on track with his patient history. Length of initial hospital stay. Complications. Rehabilitation. It was an agonising process, getting the information from him, and she was made to feel—deliberately, she suspected—horribly intrusive and insensitive.

'Any particular problems at the moment?' It was hard to keep the relief out of her voice as she neared the end of her list of questions.

Before Mr North could respond Lee appeared in the doorway. 'Have you remembered our carer skills group, Karen? Due to start in five minutes.'

'Might be a bit late,' she told him. 'Tell Maggie and Louise to start without me.'

'I'm doing it today instead of Maggie,' Lee said. 'But, OK, we will start. Problem here?' His glance flicked towards the new admission, and Karen knew that he would have picked up on the man's hostility at once.

'Problem?' Ross North laughed derisively. 'You try recounting every sordid detail of your so-called "patient history" for the hundredth time and decide if it's a problem. But, no, I know what you mean. Have I got a bladder infection or an ingrown toe-nail or a bedsore? Matter of fact, I have. Nice little sore on my left hip here from staying in bed because there was no bloody point in getting up! Not that I can feel a thing, but Jill's been at me about it as usual.'

'A pressure sore?' Lee said, exchanging another glance with Karen. It was one of the main topics of today's carer skills group.

'I don't want a lecture,' Ross North growled, closing his eyes. 'I know what causes them, what prevents them, how dangerous they can be and what cures them. I know there's no reason why, with proper care and management, any paraplegic should develop decubitus ulcers—as they are more properly called, blah, blah, blah.' He parroted the phrases, grimly parodying the cheerful, clinical tone of the pamphlets he would have been given on self-care.

'Well, since you know all that,' Lee challenged him briskly, 'could I ask you to come and help demonstrate it at the group I'm about to run?'

'Eh?' Mr North looked taken aback.

'I need a guinea-pig. You sound like the ideal volunteer.'

'Oh, hell, it never ends, does it?' he groaned. 'OK, I set myself up for that, didn't I?'

'Then you'll come along?'

'As if I had a choice!'

'Well, you *do* actually,' Lee said mildly. 'I'm not about to force you to have your hip—or your soul—bared before an avid audience.'

'Oh, go ahead. What do I care?'

Seeing that Ross North's agreement was never going to be gracious, Lee merely shrugged and took hold of the wheelchair. It was a clumsy, old-fashioned model without special controls, Karen noted, and she was surprised. Ross North had a cervical 6 lesion—meaning that the damage to his spinal cord was at the level of one of the lower neck vertebrae, and this gave him a good deal of upper-arm mobility, as well as some use of his wrists. A good wheelchair would markedly increase the number of things he could do for himself, but this one offered him only the possibility of very clumsy movement.

Lee had evidently made this same assessment and
manoeuvred the quadriplegic as far as the door of the
room, then stopped. Karen watched and waited. Mr North
could and should take over at this point. He didn't.

'OK, Mr North,' Lee prompted.

'Don't ''Mister'' me. It's Ross, all right? That goes
for all of you.' He glanced sourly at Karen.

'Ross, then. This whole complex is fully wheelchair-
accessible, so. . .'

'You do it. I'm tired. Bloody thing.'

'You could use an electric model.'

'Yeah, with controls for this and controls for that.
''Self-feeding is even a possibility.'' ' Again there was
that mocking parody of the information booklets he had
been given to read over the past two years. He went on,
'Next you'll be wanting me to start doing floral arrange-
ments with my teeth, like all those bloody therapists at
the hospital rehab centre. God, I'll murder Jill for making
me come here. I told her. . .'

The rest of the tirade faded away as Lee, without
another word, took the handles at the back of the wheelchair and began to push again. Karen took a controlled
breath and noted down the pressure sore that Mr North. . .
Ross. . .had mentioned then read through the notes she
had taken, as well as the assessment report Linwood had
received from the community nursing team.

The report presented no surprises. Rather, it gave more
depth to the initial impression that Ross North and his
wife had given. The man was angry and depressed about
his state, apathetic about efforts towards independence
in the activities of daily living and his marriage seemed
to be in serious trouble. He would be at Linwood for
three weeks while his wife took a break—'much needed',
the assessment report said—and there was some doubt
expressed as to whether she would be willing to resume
her caring role.

Karen sighed and bundled the notes away in their folder, then returned them to the nursing office. She wondered whether Lee had been wise to suggest using Ross North as a model for his session on pressure sores. They tried to keep these teaching groups upbeat. . .

The group had gathered and the session was under way by the time Karen arrived. There were quite a number of participants today, mostly in pairs of patient and carer—although some people were attending alone. Karen recognised Harry Makepeace's wife, and was pleased to see that Mary Thomas was here as well.

In the centre of the circle was Ross North, still looking hostile and reluctant. 'I suppose you want me to strip down and take off the dressing?'

'No, Ross, I don't think we need to actually view the villain of the piece,' Lee said cheerfully, 'but perhaps you could tell us about it. Obviously you'll need help with it while you're here but that's a nursing matter and, believe it or not, we do give you some privacy!'

For a moment Ross looked almost disappointed, as if he'd been looking forward to the chance of some sympathy. He muttered, 'Tell them about it? What do you want me to say?'

'How long you've had it, how your routines broke down to allow it to develop and how you're treating it now.'

Ross North turned down his mouth. 'Hell, I'll be giving a bloody lecture!'

He glared at everyone. Some people looked uncomfortable but Mrs Makepeace, who was quite used to being glared at by husband Harry, simply glared back more forcefully and this seemed to prompt Ross into speech at last.

'Well, of course, I wish now I hadn't let it get out of hand,' he began. 'That's the trouble, really—you can't forget about the wretched things. They're always there, like, like. . .I don't know, hungry wolves lurking just beyond the firelight.' It was a surprisingly vivid image. 'You have to keep vigilant every hour of every day to keep them at bay. . .'

'I think that went pretty well, don't you?' Lee said to Karen an hour later as the session broke up.

'It certainly did.' She glanced over at Ross North, who was propelling his wheelchair across the room with considerably more energy than he had shown earlier.

He had spoken fluently in the end, about shifting weight regularly—whether sitting or lying—to restore circulation to areas under pressure; about the danger of hard objects such as keys in a pocket or even rough seams in clothing which could chafe the skin, and about ways to pack and protect vulnerable areas. He had finished with the exhortation, 'Don't let yourself or your partner—mother, whoever—forget to watch for danger signs, because you'll be sorry if you do.'

Lee had then stepped in to give a demonstration of lifting a wheelchair-bound person in order to relieve pressure, and Karen had talked about the kit that should be kept on hand at home for the treating of any minor knocks or scrapes.

Towards the end of the session the floor had been thrown open for other concerns, and Mary Thomas had said firmly, 'I want to learn self-cath while I'm here.' She used a common shorthand for the technique of emptying the bladder by catheterising it at regular intervals each day, and Lee explained briefly what she meant as there were some questioning looks.

'Hopefully, when this exacerbation passes,' Mrs Thomas continued, 'I won't need it again for a good while, but this seems like a good opportunity to get the technique down to a fine art for ongoing use in later years. Will that be possible?'

'It certainly will,' Lee had told her. 'Karen. . .?'

'We'll start this afternoon,' she promised Mary. 'It does take a fair bit of practice and care, especially for women.'

Now Mary Thomas had struck up a conversation with Mrs Makepeace. Ross North glanced at them on his way out and his face fell back into its customary hostile lines. Karen wondered what he was thinking, and Lee echoed something of her own perception.

'No easy answers. We gave him a bit of a prod this afternoon, but that's not enough. I'd have liked to talk to his wife.'

'The assessment report said his marriage was in trouble,' Karen replied. 'She's gone away, apparently.'

But she hadn't. Half an hour later, after giving Mrs Thomas her first lesson in self-catheterisation, Karen glanced in the direction of Lee's office as she came down the corridor and saw Jill North, outside the door, looking nervous and uncertain. Catching up to the pretty, dark-haired woman quickly, she asked, 'Is there something I can help you with, Mrs North?'

'Is Ross around? I—I don't want him to know I'm here. I had to talk to someone. I'm getting a later train now.'

'Ross *is* around.' In fact, he was in the dining-room further along the corridor, having his afternoon tea. 'Is our manager not in?'

'I—I haven't tried. Would he be the right person? He must be busy. . .'

'Not too busy,' Karen said firmly, 'and neither am I.'

She knocked on Lee's door and he gave his usual informal, 'Yup!' He was striding around busily filing papers with a bang of the cabinet drawers, but stopped and gave them his full attention as soon as they entered.

'This is Mrs North, Lee. She wants to talk to us about Ross.'

With the three of them closeted in the office and the door closed, Jill North was soon in tears. 'Married thirteen years before the accident, very happily, and now, suddenly, over the past two years I'm feeling he must have hooked me in under false pretences and he's only just revealing his true self. Which is so ridiculous! Of course it isn't that deliberate on his part! I know what he must be going through. I want to stick it out. I do! But I'm starting to doubt that I can. It's so horrible!'

'What are your plans at the moment?' Lee asked. 'You're going away, aren't you?'

'You mean, "And am I coming back?" I don't know! You're right. There's a chance I might not, and yet I've always believed that the vow I made "for better, for worse," should be unbreakable. Don't you think?'

'If you feel that, and it can be incentive enough for you, then—'

'No, Mr Shadwell. I'm not asking you to affirm my feelings—to nod supportively at whatever I say. I want to know what you think you'd do in my position.'

'About that vow? About sticking it out?' He spread his hands. 'Like you, I'd want to try my hardest. I'm not married, but if I did marry I hope I'd have the courage to make that commitment and follow through on it.'

His eyes flicked to Karen briefly and darted away again, and she felt the tension rising in her—tightening her muscles until they ached. She was already thinking of Paul, trying to reconsider her relationship with him as Megan Stone had asked her to do and wondering if she should have stuck it out.

Here was a patient's wife wrestling with the same issue and now Lee was quietly stating his belief that one should 'follow through', looking at her as if he knew that, with Paul, she hadn't done so. He *didn't* know, of course, and he must not.

'You think it comes down to courage?' Jill North was

saying. 'Perhaps. And perhaps I haven't got it.'

'Mrs North, I—' Lee began.

'Look, I won't take any more of your time. I—I must get away—away from Camberton—and think it all out properly.'

'Don't feel that—' Lee tried again, but she was already in the doorway, dabbing at her tear-stained eyes with a scrap of tissue and fumbling in her bag for car keys.

'I'm glad I've put you in the picture as to what's going on,' she said briskly. 'Thank you for taking the time.'

She set off down the corridor before Karen or Lee could speak again, and the latter shrugged expressively. Karen, though, was in the grip of anger. It had ambushed her unexpectedly—a natural reaction, perhaps, to the strain of the past couple of days, but she was beyond that sort of rational analysis and blurted, 'Do you think it was right to question her courage and commitment like that? When we know so little of her situation? To make her feel judged?'

His face dropped and his glance was sharp, reminding her suddenly that gold-flecked brown eyes didn't always look warm. 'I wasn't judging her, Karen.'

'No? With your paean to the sacred nature of those vows? She's gone away feeling weak and inadequate which, I'd have thought, is not the best frame of mind in which to make the right decision about her future.'

She saw that she had succeeded in rousing him to anger now too and was perversely pleased at the fact, without fully knowing why. Needing the release, perhaps? Or the safety of some distance and dissent between them?

'Don't you think you're overreacting a little?' he said, the mild words deceptive. His well-drawn mouth was tight. 'She pressed for my personal opinion and I gave it honestly. I *do* hope I'd stick it out. And, as it happens,

I *do* think that many people give up on their marriages far too easily these days.'

'Just marriages?'

'Marriages, engagements. . . What's your point?'

'Is it the breaking of the vows you object to, Lee? The breaking of someone's publicly given word?' She didn't quite know why she was pressing him like this.

'Not entirely. But isn't this just quibbling?' His impatience was growing. 'As I was going to say—when I realised she'd taken my words as an indictment of her courage I did try to reassure her, but you saw what happened. She left.'

'Yes, you're right, of course.'

She controlled the sigh which threatened to gust through the words as she realised that her cryptic questioning was asking for the impossible. She needed him to tell her that she owed Paul Chambers nothing and certainly not a rekindling of their relationship.

But Lee couldn't tell her any such thing and if she had angered him—quenched the brief attraction he had felt for her—well, so much the better. It was one less complication.

An hour later, directly after work, she caught the bus into the city centre and bought the books she had promised to get for Paul, then decided that she might as well deliver them to him now. He was bored, and would value the entertainment they could provide.

'Perhaps I can find the courage and commitment, even if it's without love. Perhaps I should. If Dr Stone is right. . . Perhaps Paul does want to make some changes.'

But the whole thing nagged at her, a churning sea of conflicting emotions that she didn't trust or understand at all, and she hated the looming view of Camberton Hospital as it rose on the hill before her when she stepped down from the bus.

CHAPTER FIVE

THE crowded grounds of Camberthorpe Castle churned with colour and noise at noon on Saturday when Karen and Susie arrived for the Youth Arts League Medieval Festival, both dressed comfortably in shorts, sandals and cotton blouses.

'My goodness, it's splendiferous, isn't it?' Susie exclaimed, darting her pert dark head around to take everything in. 'I've never been here before. In fact, I've never known it to be open to the public before.'

'It's changed hands over the past couple of years, apparently,' Karen said, repeating the explanation that Lee had given her. 'And the new American owners were very generous about making it available this afternoon. I think we can even tour the castle itself for another pound.'

Susie wasn't keen. 'You'd have to pay *me* a pound at least to get me out of this sunshine when I've only got until two-thirty!'

She had an afternoon shift at the hospital later on so they decided to have lunch straight away, before exploring the other options for entertainment.

Winding her way through the crowds behind impatient 'starving' Susie, Karen couldn't help looking for Lee. She kept catching glimpses of a bright head of hair above the throngs, then would decide, No, that man's too fair, with the same absurd mixture of reprieve and disappointment that she'd been feeling at work over the past few days whenever she narrowly missed him in the staffroom or the nursing office.

After some minutes of this she realised, I probably

won't see him at all. He'll be tucked away somewhere, counting gate-takings or trouble-shooting over some crisis. It was naïve to assume I'd just run into him.

She put him out of her mind with real relief.

If there was a man for her thoughts to dwell on, then it should be Paul. Each day this past week she had gone up to the hospital to see him and each day he had been disturbingly quiescent, seeming poignantly pleased to see her. He did not seem the same man who had captured her heart so cynically and so deliberately last year, but a man who seemed to deserve her concern nonetheless.

He had her tied in knots as she wondered, Which is the real Paul? I want to do the right thing, but where does rightness lie? I don't love him. I can see now that I never did, but do I owe him the commitment I thought I was making last year?

Megan Stone hadn't helped yesterday afternoon— although it wasn't her fault—by her evident approval of Karen's visits.

'He's been much easier to handle since you started coming. Do keep it up if you can!'

Karen had nodded, hiding her agonising ambivalence. 'I'll be here again tomorrow, late in the afternoon.'

She planned to go straight from this fair, in fact, per- haps with some silly purchase for him from one of the craft or produce stalls.

Susie sniffed the air like a human bloodhound. 'We're getting close, and I can hear a sizzle, I'm sure. Oh, I *hope* it's not too crowded! I slept till nearly eleven and didn't have breakfast. . . Ooh, look, spit-roasted meats, turnip soup, bread straight out of the wood-fired oven. . . and there isn't even much of a queue!'

At Susie's insistence they opted for the entire 'Medieval Banquet Platter' which was on offer and sat, eating it, at one of the long wooden trestle tables—now rapidly filling up—which commanded an impressive view of the jousting demonstration.

With Susie in a far more tractable state now that the demon hunger had been appeased, they then browsed the various stalls, buying herbal remedies—Susie chose a love potion—potted jams and hand-woven place-mats, and ran briefly across fellow Linwood personnel Alison Parker and Heather Lewis.

The fortune-teller's tent was fun, too. A witch of a teenager, who had to be the rising star of the Youth Arts League's drama group—to judge from her considerable talent—told each of them a thickly embroidered tale of unexpected income, peril-fraught voyaging and handsome millionaire strangers.

Susie was delighted with this final promise, but Karen instinctively shook her head and the teenager, 'Mistress Dominie', fixed her with a perceptive and glittering dark stare and intoned, 'Ah, ye want not part of it, but the wind will change direction, mark ye, my lady, as sure as spring turns to summer, I promise ye!'

'Oh, do ye—I mean, do you?' Karen muttered sceptically. 'Er, thanks.'

'Aye, mark ye well my words! It will blow from a fresh quarter across sweet-flowered pastures and strew your path with—' At this point, Mistress Dominie suddenly broke off, apparently catching sight of a movement through a loosely laced gap in the tent walls, and called out eagerly, 'Lee? Oh, Lee? Wait, can't you?'

There was a movement of the tent flap behind them and Lee entered, grimacing at the rather mildewed smell of the canvas. The fortune-teller leaped to her feet with a rustle of her billowing skirts.

'You said once I'd got over fifty quid in my tin I had to get Mark to take it up to the committee tent,' she said to him, all trace of Mistress Dominie gone, 'but he's disappeared, and I'm doing a roaring trade and I must have at least seventy-five in here by now.'

She stopped suddenly and clapped her be-ringed hand over her mouth, turning to Karen and Susie. 'Oh, my goodness! I dropped *completely* out of role! I'm *so* sorry!'

'It doesn't matter,' Karen said and shifted on her shawl-draped stool to greet Lee, who was blinking as his brown eyes adjusted to the dimmer light.

'Seventy-five?' he said. 'That's great! I'll take it up to the tent myself, then, and just leave you enough to give change. I wonder what's happened to Mark, though.'

'You haven't seen him either?'

'Not since about one-ish.' His half-turn towards Karen seemed casual and very distracted. 'Glad you could come. . .'

'Oh, we're enjoying—' Karen began eagerly.

But he was already involved in practicalities again, hefting the open cash box from behind the fortune teller's draped table. Karen could have kicked herself. What was she expecting? The red-carpet treatment? Come off it!

'Had you finished, Mistress Dominie?' Susie asked.

'Oh, pretty much. But I ruined it for you at the end there,' the girl answered with ingenuous regret. 'You can have your money back, if you like.'

'Nonsense!' Susie said kindly. 'You were wonderful! I'm dying to see what Karen's "fresh wind" is going to bring!'

'Probably a draught under my door and rheumatism in my joints,' Karen drawled, still in cynical mode, and they left Mistress Dominie with her eyes closed, meditating herself back 'into role', while Lee rattled her cash box and crossed his own palm with a considerable quantity of silver.

'I'll have to go, Karen,' Susie said regretfully outside in the bright daylight once more. 'It's nearly twenty past two already, and it's got so crowded now I'll probably take quite a while just to get to the gate. Tell me what the castle's like if you pay your pound to see inside. I love hearing how the other two per cent lives.'

'Two per cent?'

'If it really was "the other half", I'd have a better chance of marrying one, wouldn't I?'

'According to Mistress Dominie, you can just rest on your laurels and wait for it to happen.'

'Do you think she'd give me a weekly session? If she intones it often enough in that hypnotic language, perhaps it'll come true!'

They parted on a laugh and Susie was lost to sight in seconds. The place *was* crowded now, everyone lured by the twin prospects of spring sunshine and a castle open for viewing after years of being private to the point of mystery. It would be interesting to see. . .

But then Lee emerged from the tent, canvas coin-bag jingling, and said casually, 'I'm due for a break, I think, once I've taken this loot up to the committee tent. Need some company, you and. . .Susie was it? I haven't had a chance to actually see what's going on here yet.'

'Susie's gone. Had to work,' Karen explained.

'Just you, then.'

Their eyes met, a clash of brown and blue, and if Karen had been kidding herself over the past few days that she'd got the little matter of her sudden and inconvenient attraction to Lee Shadwell fully under control, then she couldn't kid herself any longer. On this bright day, with the hectic distraction of Linwood and work no longer a camouflage, it flared into life again—like the dormant coals of a fire, fanned by the wind.

What was worse was that he was feeling it too, and they both knew it. In fact, so much was communicated by the brief meeting of their eyes that Karen had to stare away—down, anywhere—to regain her cool.

'Let's go,' he said lightly.

He threaded his way through the crowds up to the

committee tent, and her heart was lurching quite drunk-enly as she followed him.

'This is going to be quite a gratifying success,' he predicted, lifting his bright head to survey the crowded stalls and demonstration areas, from where he stood beside Karen on the rise just below the castle walls. 'Thanks to the weather! What have you seen?'

'Not half of it, I don't think,' Karen said. 'Susie was starving so we banqueted for a good while.'

'Did you?' An expression appeared on his face not unlike that of a wolf's at the end of a harsh winter.

'You haven't, I take it?'

'Someone did bring me something a couple of hours ago.'

'So what are you complaining about? Delicious, I hope?'

'A piece of charred venison in some underdone bread, gory with tomato sauce.'

'Aagh!' They both knew that something was going on beneath this banter.

'And the sauce isn't even authentic!' he complained.

'Saving the good stuff for the paying guests?' she suggested.

'Quite right, really, and yet. . .'

'Oh Lee, you always sound so *mournful* when you're hungry and talking about food,' she laughed, giving in at last to a pure enjoyment of his company. 'Here's a stall just here, selling apple turnovers and plum tarts and things. Shall I provision you while you're doing finances and meet you back here?'

'Ah! What a fine idea!' He was brisk now. 'Two turn-overs, please, and. . .are those lemon tarts? Two of those as well.' He thrust some notes into her hand.

'You're worse than Susie!'

'Susie. . . A woman I instinctively warm to, since she clearly shares my appreciation of the medical fact that caloric energy expended must be replaced as soon as possible or muscular degeneration and the depletion of reserve fat deposits will result.'

'You don't have any reserve fat deposits, Lee.'

'I'm working on it,' he assured her.

'Clearly! Are you sure you can manage two turnovers *and* two tarts?'

'Quite sure, thanks.'

He grinned and disappeared into the crowd so she joined the queue for the pie stall and bought the things he had asked for, seeing him come towards her just as she had completed her purchases. He grinned again, and only then did she realise that she still wore the same foolish smile that his humour had provoked several minutes ago.

'So, what *haven't* you seen?' He was brisk and cheerful, the golden glints in his brown eyes bright in the strong sunlight.

'The medieval dancing, the archery and all the stalls along the west side. Nor the castle itself.'

'I won't have time for that,' he said, and she interrupted hastily.

'Oh, I didn't mean. . .I'm not expecting to take up your whole afternoon.'

'You could, with pleasure,' he murmured gallantly, and she knew, as he wanted her to, that he meant it, 'if I had the time, but the committee's demands are relentless.'

As if to underline this statement he was hailed at that moment by a burgundy-haired woman of about thirty-eight in decidedly un-medieval hot-pink leggings, heavy make-up, enormous jangly earrings and a black knitted top with a neckline that drooped rather too low across her full, freckle-dappled breasts.

'Lee, *have* you seen Mark?' She came up to him and laid a beseeching talon-nailed hand on his bare forearm.

'No, I'm off with Karen, here, to look for him now.'

The woman frowned at Karen, her very female antenna picking up signals. Then she bit her lip. 'I'm *so* sorry, Lee. You thought he wouldn't want the responsibility, and it looks as if you were *quite* right.'

'There's no proof of that yet, Melody,' Lee soothed, accepting her anxious caresses without actually responding to them. She was plucking at his rust-coloured shirt-front now, her pink nails clicking.

'*No one's* seen him!' Not a tall woman, her upward glance emphasised his own height and strength of bearing.

'You think he's gone off with some of the cash?' Lee's strongly drawn brows arrowed into a heavy line.

She shrugged. 'Well. . .'

'I don't think that's his style, so let's not panic yet.'

'No, you're right, of course.' A touch on his neck, which feathered the smooth hair that ended there, underlined her gesture. 'But if you could check the archery area first?'

'Yes, I expect that would be a draw for Mark and Michael. Karen?'

'Whatever you need to do, Lee,' she assured him. 'You needn't treat me as your guest.'

Melody frowned across at her again and murmured, not looking at Lee, 'We need you here, though, desperately. I'm sorry, I know you're overdue for a break. . .! Don't be gone for hours, will you?'

'Half an hour at the most,' he soothed again.

Melody disappeared back into the tent with a fast, sinuous stride that caused several pieces of her anatomy and clothing to jiggle or sway flamboyantly, and Lee said, as if in explanation of the whole phenomenon, 'Melody's very theatrical. Melody Piper. She was quite a well-known actress for a while, and leads our drama group now. Does it very well.'

'Oh, I'm sure,' Karen answered politely.

But Lee had already dismissed Melody, it seemed. He seized Karen's hand and began to pull her rapidly in the direction of the stalls she hadn't yet browsed, as if determined to shake off responsibility for a short, precious time, and she felt the silky slide of his thumb across the backs of her fingers before he took a stronger grip and engulfed her whole hand in his warmth.

She couldn't help answering the pressure of his grip. Such a chaste gesture, holding hands, but it didn't feel that way today. On the contrary, the link that it forged between them seemed to symbolise something much stronger and she wondered, Should I pull away? That would be so petty, wouldn't it? Especially when this feels so good.

And so she stayed beside him, aware of him constantly and marvelling at the silky, syrupy colours that the sun's rays brought out in his fragrantly clean hair. The fabric of his sand-coloured pants rippled as he moved, hinting at the capable musculature beneath and spreading just right across his perfectly firm male behind. His rust shirt was made of cool, stone-washed cotton and she felt its sleeve brush her bare arm as he stopped in front of a stall.

'Herbal potions?' he suggested.

'More of them?' she groaned.

'That particular theme's been a bit overdone, has it?'

'I think every cottage herbalist for miles around has zeroed in on the opportunity,' she told him. 'See. . .' she held up her woven peasant-style carry-bag '. . .I've already got a cold remedy and a foot balm.'

'Very suitable for a nurse,' he commented drily.

She laughed. 'Oh, it is isn't it! For my chronically aching feet and exposure to every germ going. I hadn't even thought!'

'How about something on the darker side, then?' he suggested as they moved on to the next stall. 'A make-your-own wax doll kit, complete with genuine, powerful incantations and pins to stick in it. Or this salve— ''Rub it into your enemy's shoes and within nine days he will walk out of your life forever.'' '

Karen shivered. 'Actually, that's all a bit nasty. This one's made of real crushed mouse bones, supposedly.'

'It is nasty, isn't it?' he agreed. 'Though she's doing a roaring business, I notice. Look, how about this, then?'

He moved on again, dropped her hand and put an arm over her shoulder so that she felt his warmth and his male scent still more intimately around her—as luxurious and welcoming as a satin-lined cloak.

'This?' she echoed lightly.

'Not very authentic, perhaps,' he commented. 'It should be a ducking in the pond, or a set of stocks in the town market-place.'

Four teenage boys and girls had their faces pressed through holes cut in a luridly painted plywood screen, and were acting as targets for sopping sponges. A wiry young tout, evidently another star from Melody Piper's drama group to judge from his enthusiastic performance, was drawing in passers-by with promises that they could, 'Let fly in the face of these foul witches and wizards, my lords and ladies! Ye shall thereby squelch their wickedness and win for ye selves wondrous gifts from far-off lands!'

'Hmm. . . Far-off lands?' Lee murmured, picking up a tawdry pink stuffed bear. She felt the whisper of his breath against her hair. 'Made in Taiwan doesn't quite have the right allure these days, does it? Want to try? This is one of our own stalls, not a rented-out concession like most of those herbalists, so all the money will support. . .in this case. . .the drama group.'

'Oh, but they look miserable!' she winced.

'No, they don't! They're loving it. They're grimacing so violently because they're being witches, but most they can't manage to keep it up.' And, as if to confirm his theory, a red-headed girl grinned broad as she got a wet, smelly sponge full in her nose.

'Six hits and you win a prize,' the young tout told Karen, sensing that she was weakening, and Lee forked over some coins and thus decided the issue for her.

'I won't really try and hit them,' she muttered to him. 'That lass on the right is putting on a brave face, but look at her! She's scowling and her lips are going blue! And I don't really want to take one of their precious prizes. People won't play if the prizes have all disappeared.'

'Softy!' he teased, tucking into his second apple turnover, and then he watched, grinning, as she carefully and deliberately aimed for a spot a good two feet away from the poor, blue-lipped girl—and hit her full in the face. 'Changed your mind and got aggressive, I see,' he suggested evilly.

'No!' she snarled. 'Really! I *don't* want to hit them, and I wasn't aiming there at all!'

This time she aimed still further away—and hit the 'foul wizard' next along.

'Keep this up and you'll soon be the proud possessor of that fluffy purple dog.'

'Honestly, I'm not trying. . .'

'I know, you kind-hearted thing, and that's what makes it so funny!'

He was laughing openly now and Karen gritted her teeth stubbornly, unimpressed by those even white teeth and the silky slip of his hair as he tossed it back. It was ridiculous! This time she would *not* score a direct hit!

Three minutes later, having aimed as badly as she possibly could, she was slinking away from the stall with the least offensive of the stuffed animals wedged beneath her arm and the man at her side still shaking with laughter. For several more seconds Karen was furious with him, then the funny side of it struck her too. 'I should take up pub darts as a second career, shouldn't I?' she drawled, 'as long as I aim anywhere *but* at the board. . .'

'You'd make a fortune,' he promised her very seriously, and they were still laughing, arm in arm, when they reached the archery display area where the local archery club had been roped in to give demonstrations of their own skills, as well as charging a small fee for a closely supervised practice shoot to anyone who was interested.

The club had taken on the medieval theme with enthusiasm, and there was a motley and colourful array of thick hose, leather jerkins and even some chain-mail. However, just now, to Karen's disappointment they were taking a lunch-break, tucking into pork pies with an authentic medieval disregard for table manners.

A couple of teenagers, both dark, freckled and rather scrawny in appearance, had clearly been delegated to supervise the equipment and keep children well away from the target area, and Lee focused on one of them and gave a satisfied exclamation. 'Mark! Good! He hasn't absconded with the takings at all. And Michael, too.'

Seconds later, though, he wasn't so pleased, muttering under his breath, 'My God! What on earth is he doing?' He broke away from Karen's side, and she immediately craved his touch again.

With the real archers absorbed in eating and answering some questions about their sport from several bystanders, Mark and his friend had obviously got bored, and started horsing around with the equipment. Karen even wondered, as she got closer in Lee's wake, whether they had been drinking. Mark's aim was certainly nearly as bad as hers had been at—

'God! *No*!' Lee's frantic shout aroused the other archers, but it was too late. With his judgement distorted by laughter and tomfoolery, Mark had unleashed his arrow but, instead of springing towards the distant target, it had clipped the other youth hard in the side of the chest and he dropped with frightening suddenness to the ground like a fatally wounded bird.

Lee was already sprinting, grim-faced, towards the pair. Mark was on his knees, groaning with terror and remorse. He only looked about sixteen. Karen's legs were frozen and immobile for what seemed like an absurd interval but it could only have been a few seconds as she caught up with Lee only moments after he had dropped to the moaning figure on the ground.

'Lee?'

He understood at once her urgent use of his name. 'Yes!' He looked up at her from his position on the ground, his jaw square and his brown eyes compelling as they betrayed the rapid working of his mind.

'There's an emergency medical room just beyond the committee tent—inside the castle itself. He needs an ambulance, and I'm not moving him until it gets here. The arrow's lodged in his lung, from what I can see, and it might have clipped something even more vital. Bring some gear straight back down. I don't have to tell you what we might need.

'Get Melody and at least two others to wait by the main gate, with megaphones, for the ambulance. As soon as they hear it approaching they're to start clearing the crowds off the driveway, and direct the ambulance here across the lawns.'

She nodded and was off, as Lee began an urgent round of questions and instructions to both Mark and his injured friend. 'Where does it hurt? How is your breathing? Move as little as you can. I'm going to place your limbs more comfortably for you. Please don't try and move yourself. I'm going to cut away your shirt with this pocket knife, OK? Don't be frightened; you're going to be all right. . .'

Even at a sprint, Karen's progress through the crowd seemed frustratingly slow as she had to dodge around milling groups of people at the stalls. Word had already spread about the dramatic accident and the more ghoulish of the fair-goers were asking each other, 'Do you want to go and see? An arrow sticking out of his chest? Cor! Which way is the archery demo?'

At the castle she found the medical room easily, led to it by the loud cries of an injured child, and found the two nurses in attendance both up to their eyeballs with a badly bumped and cut head, a twisted knee and three elderly people for whom the sunshine, the crowds and the wailing had all proved too much.

'Take what you need,' they told her, after checking her credentials. 'And get Mrs Piper or Mr Hebden to page for a doctor. There must be one here in all this mob.'

Karen phoned for the ambulance, giving the sketchy details she knew, and threw together a variety of dressings and swabs, antiseptic, syringes, needles and one or two of the more likely drugs, as well as equipment for setting up a drip and fluids.

In the committee tent Melody Piper was loudly aghast and in a flap. 'My God, we'll be sued! My God, a *doctor*? Yes. . . The ambulance? Megaphones? Who can we spare? Jack? David?'

'Spare anyone,' Karen suggested crisply. 'It's a serious injury.'

She didn't wait for the conclusion to Mrs Piper's emotional deliberations but picked up her medical equipment in its bulky metal box and raced back down to the archery area. Tried to race. Seeing the red cross on the box she carried, people attempted to get out of her way. A man offered to help but she didn't quite dare to trust a stranger with these urgently needed things so she arrived finally very breathless, and with a bruise already swelling on her leg from where the sharp corner of the metal had bumped it persistently as she ran.

'Thank God!' Lee said to her in a terse, private aside.

He seemed very different now from the lazy, laughing man who had teased her about her prowess with the wet sponges and she realised that, in her seven weeks at Linwood, she hadn't yet seen him fully in the grip of an emergency of this scale.

His whole body, already commanding in its athleticism, looked harder, more angular and powerful. His jaw was jutting and determined, and the delicate skin around his gold-flecked brown eyes looked tight as he narrowed them in rapid calculation.

Even his voice was subtly different—controlled, confident, and completely authoritative—as he told people to stand back and he used it almost like a strait-jacket on distraught Mark, keeping him from hysteria by sheer force of will.

'It's a tension pneumothorax,' he said to Karen. A serious tear in the lung, she knew at once, letting air escape internally. 'And that air pressure is building dangerously in the chest cavity, compressing the lungs so that they'll be useless soon. I've got to relieve the pressure. You brought. . .?'

'Yes, a large-bore needle.' She was already opening the box.

'Good!' The single syllable expressed a wealth of feeling. 'No doctor?'

'Melody is paging for one.'

'Useless, I suspect. That loudspeaker system is practically unintelligible. Now, as soon as I've relieved this pressure—' He was working as he spoke.

'It'll build again, won't it?'

'Yes,' Lee nodded. 'I won't be able to let up on this till he's in hospital with the proper equipment. Every breath he takes leaks more air into the cavity. He's exhausted with the effort already. He's bleeding, and I don't dare remove that arrow or even cut off the shaft in case I dislodge it. If it's acting as a plug to stop more dangerous bleeding. . .'

'Or if, in moving it, you nick something vital. . .'

'Exactly, so I'll need you to bandage the arrow and immobilise it against his chest and arm, as if you were splinting an extra limb. . . Now, Michael?' He turned to their patient, speaking loudly and crisply to distract the injured teenager's attention away from effort and pain. Meanwhile, Mark was being kept at a distance, almost sobbing with remorse and being soothed by an older couple. Karen quietly suggested that he be taken up to the medical room for a sedative and a lie-down.

'Hold on for a moment, man, don't breathe,' Lee was saying. 'I'm going to release that pressure and you'll feel a lot better.'

The agonising labour of the youth's breathing ceased as Lee swabbed the bony ribs with antiseptic and inserted the thick needle to release a whistling gush of air that seemed to continue for minutes, although it must have been much less than that.

'Oh, wow, I can breathe, I can breathe,' Michael groaned and took in gulped lungfuls of air, which immediately began to start the process of pressure building again. 'But the pain is still. . .'

'The ambulance is on its way.'

The arrow was a sickening sight, its shaft disappearing into the teenager's side through a messy, bloody hole. It was like some bad cowboy movie, only it was far too real. Karen bound it tightly between his arm and chest, using every piece of gauze and tape and elastic bandage she could find in her box, while Lee managed to fit up a drip—balancing the precious bag of fluid on top of the metal kit box.

'No doctor yet,' he muttered. 'And I will say. . .bullets make cleaner holes. He's tiring fast. . .'

They heard the ambulance at last, its siren brash in the middle of a bright afternoon, startling those who hadn't yet heard of the accident. The crowds pressed back and there were some murmurs of shame and distaste. 'Fancy *watching*! Ghouls! And getting in the way. . .'

Melody Piper strode up, breathless, her too-lavish breasts heaving and her earrings jangling. 'How is he? Oh, it's Michael.'

'He'll make it.' Lee was terse, wasting no words—a statement of his faith rather than his certainty.

Michael was on the stretcher now with Lee as close as he could get, holding the drip bag high and watching the taped arrow and the taped needle carefully to make sure that they didn't shift.

'. . .because things are falling apart without you.' It was a tremulous wail from Melody, and Lee didn't bother to disguise his impatience.

'Tough! He needs two people in the ambulance, as well as the driver, so I'll have to go.' The ambulance officers nodded.

'You *can't*!' Another wail.

'Melody. . .'

The woman's name was ominous on Lee's lips and she subsided, half whispering, half wailing to no one in particular. . .or perhaps to Karen, 'He doesn't realise. It's their job. They must be able to handle it! The hospital's only minutes away. And where's a doctor? We paged for one ages ago and we're still repeating the announcement at three-minute intervals.'

Lee climbed into the ambulance, his limbs athletic and economical in movement and his focus totally on the patient. Seconds later the vehicle was gone, siren keening again.

Karen began to pack up the equipment with hands that shook slightly, and heard Melody's tetchy and tear-fogged voice above her. '*You* could have gone! If Lee had only waited a moment we would have thought of it!'

'He's far more experienced than I am,' Karen said. 'And he felt responsible. . .as I'm sure you did.' Would Melody take the hint?

Evidently not. The woman was behaving terribly! She moaned, 'Oh, it's too terrible, too stupid. *Wretched* Mark! The whole thing was handled badly, and if there are costs and it eats up all the profits so I can't do my production of *Romeo and Juliet*. . .' A mascara-stained tear disappeared into her freckled cleavage.

Karen could only dismiss the irrelevant problem with a coolly polite smile and then, as she picked up her heavy metal box ready to return it to the medical room, she saw a faintly familiar figure pushing through the still-gathered onlookers.

'I'm a doctor. I heard one was needed.'

'Too late,' Karen told him ruefully. 'Thanks, though.'

'That sound system. . . It took three repeats of the announcement before I understood it. What happened?'

'The ambulance has just left.'

'Ah. I was touring the castle. Didn't hear it through those ancient walls. Serious, then?'

'Yes. . .' She was trying to place him. Camberton Hospital, she was sure. Surgeon? She thought so. 'An arrow through the lung, tension pneumothorax and goodness knows what else. We didn't dare pull it out,' she explained.

'Bloody hell! They'll probably bleep me anyway, then.'

'I've seen you before, I think. You're—'

'Callum Priestley. Cardio-thoracic surgeon,' he nodded. 'Look, I'll head in. My reg isn't very experienced. I don't want her tackling this alone.'

'Can I come with you?' she blurted out, before she could regret it. 'I hate not knowing . . .' Then she held her breath. What would he think?

He had a dramatically hewn face, not unattractive, incredibly strong but quite forbidding, until. . .'Sure!' he smiled. 'I know what you mean.' And she decided that she liked him.

Fifteen minutes later, after she had returned the medical equipment and met Mr Priestley and his car at the main gate, she was hurrying into Accident and Emergency in his wake—only to see him whisked away by a nurse who filled him in at once on the details in a clipped, professional way. There was no sign of Lee, and the nursing staff were unfamiliar to her.

'The patient has gone straight into surgery,' they reported to Karen. 'No more news yet.'

And there had been a boating accident with two serious casualties brought in just a few minutes ago, so everyone was too frantic to be able to tell her what had happened to Lee.

She began to regret her impulsive ride-hitching with the surgeon. Perhaps I'd have been more use to poor selfish Mrs Piper at the fair!

Go back? No, it was after four already. . .

She might as well visit Paul, then, since she'd planned to come up anyway, between four and six, for Saturday's visiting hours. Paul. Wrenching herself into that state of feeling again. She'd had too many changes of emotional pace in the last hour or two—Lee teasing and relaxed and deliberately sensual; Lee forcefully in control over the drama between Mark and Michael, and now. . .

She left Accident and Emergency and made her way around to the chest ward, conscious in the shade of the hospital buildings outside that the day's warmth was now past its peak and more conscious of her reluctance increasing like a weighted load as she approached Paul's room.

He was asleep. Relief and guilt mingled inside her.

She shouldn't wake him. . .but that was just an excuse. His handsome blue eyes were hooded by his closed lids; his cheeks were flushed in sleep. She couldn't help watching him for a moment, poised as still as a mouse in the doorway.

In full health, even in his mid-forties as he now was, he had always been an extraordinarily good-looking man. She had been aware of that fact since their first meeting last year, and when she had first lost her heart to him and known that they would inevitably come together she had expected automatically that the love-making of such a man would be rapturous—wonderful for her.

It hadn't been, though. She still didn't quite know why. Her fault, somehow. . . She had surrendered her purity to him in a glow of radiant emotion, and hadn't questioned her own lack of physical fulfilment at first. He was experienced. She was not. It was enough that they were together. . . And how could she expect to succeed at love's mystery straight away? He would tutor her tenderly, and soon the perfect pieces would fall into place.

But they never had, and he had rather quickly become impatient with her. She blamed herself for that and felt guilty—and relieved—on the many nights when he seemed too tired or too preoccupied with his writing to want her. Really they hadn't made love very often, she remembered, still watching him sleep. If she went back to him, as he seemed to want, would she be able to make their physical relationship work any better?

A draught came from along the corridor as someone opened a door, and suddenly she was cold and gave a shiver. Paul stirred. Karen held her breath and waited. Long seconds passed, then he settled again without opening his eyes and she ducked out of the doorway and beyond his range of vision, the muscles in her head beginning to clamp around her skull like two strong hands.

'I won't wake him. I can't see him today.'

Jill North's words the other day about 'sticking it out' came back to her, haunting and ominous.

CHAPTER SIX

THE staff nurse at the desk, whom Karen didn't know, frowned as she passed on her way out of the men's chest ward, and she explained briefly, 'Paul's asleep. I didn't want to disturb him.'

Still restless, she returned to Accident and Emergency to be told the same thing about young Michael as she had heard before. 'In surgery. No news yet.'

The she saw Lee, coming towards her along the internal corridor that led to the lifts and operating theatres. He looked strained and on edge—until he caught sight of her. Then there was a brief lightening of his expression, like the sun coming out in the middle of a cloud-shadowed field.

'How'd you get here?'

'Mr Priestley gave me a ride. He was at the fair, but he heard the paging announcement too late.'

'Top-notch surgeon,' Lee said. 'He's in there now. They let me watch from the corridor for a bit.'

'Anything. . .?'

'Too early.' He shook his head. 'The arrow's out, but it nicked an artery on the way. Unavoidable. There's some major patching-up to do. We were right not to do more than we did on site. . .' He shook off the subject and demanded, 'You've been here for a while, then?'

'I—I went up to see Paul. . .my friend who's in hospital.'

The name slipped out before she thought and settled into the air, creating a ripple of awareness between them. It wouldn't be hard for Lee to realise that Paul was. . . . *had been*. . .important to her. He was observing her narrowly—waiting, she saw, for her to say something more.

But how could she, when she didn't even know her own decision about the future? To dump a load of her uncertainties onto Lee now would be too horrible for both of them. So she stayed silent and Paul's name hung there for a little longer while they looked at each other, the space between them electric with unsaid things.

'I've got to get back to the fair,' he said at last. 'Melody was unforgivable. . .but she's right, now that there's nothing more I can do here. I *am* needed. How about you?'

She moved restlessly and blurted out, 'Look, do you need help? I'm— After what's happened this afternoon—' she meant Paul, as much as Michael's drastic accident '—I—I feel very unsettled, and if you are short-handed. . .'

'The fair ends at six,' he told her. 'We've got a crew standing by to clean up, but there'll be a couple of hours of counting takings and overseeing the whole packing-up procedure. Too boring?'

'No, not at all.'

'In that case, we'd really appreciate your help.' There was a caress in his tone but she set her jaw and ignored it, regretting the ease with which she'd responded to him today.

They took a taxi back and she spent two and a half hours in the stuffy committee tent, counting money in the greenish-hued light that filtered through the canvas and listening to the sweep and flow of activity and conversation as the fair ended and the cleaning-up took on its full momentum.

Melody Piper remained an insistent presence, her moods seeming to swing frequently and Lee's name frequently on her lips. The other male members of the committee—Jack Hebden and David Raul—didn't seem to earn her attention nearly so often.

By a quarter to eight it was done and the clean-up crew wanted to dismantle this last tent.

'We're all going to dinner, Lee, at that Chinese place on the corner of Church Street,' Melody said. 'Will we see you there?'

'Don't think so, thanks, Mel,' he answered lightly at once. 'Been quite a day. . .'

'Oh, *Lee*! But we're *celebrating*!' she wailed, going up to him and clasping her hands together beseechingly so that her deep cleavage became a tight, dark line. Her blouse had sagged considerably during the course of the afternoon, it seemed to Karen. At any second the details of her bra, or its absence, would be public knowledge. 'We made a *fortune*!'

'Yeah, and I'm sure that's important to poor young Michael Clegg right now,' muttered Jack Hebden, out of Mrs Piper's earshot.

If Lee had the same attitude he didn't let it show. He put his arms lightly on her shoulders and she reached up to him, her carefully packaged chest shaped into a provocative pout and her smile wide and creamy as she anticipated a capitulation. It didn't come.

'Melody, your production of *Romeo and Juliet* is now safely in the bag financially. You'll spend the whole evening discussing every detail of set, costumes and casting and, since the drama group is not my area of expertise, I'd only cramp your style,' he told her, gently mocking her own theatricality with his tone. 'Now. . .I'm giving Karen a lift.'

The latter raised her head, a little alarmed at being dragged into the matter. Would Mrs Piper go down without a fight? She pouted again—with her freshly painted lips this time. 'I *won't* discuss it, I promise, if you don't want me to.'

'I wouldn't dream of depriving you of the pleasure,' he responded very firmly, the glint in his brown eyes softening the words, and she subsided at last.

It was another quarter of an hour before all the good-byes and jubilant self-congratulations on the success of the day were finally made, as well as some more sober comments about injured Michael, then at last Karen was cocooned in Lee's car to hear his first words—an apology.

'I roped you into my own agenda there. Melody's like a chocolate liqueur—very rich, and best in small doses. And I hate post-mortems on these events. So, can I drop you home on my way to the hospital? Or anywhere else you want to go, for that matter.'

'You're going back to see about Michael?' she guessed. 'Yes, I expect his parents would be there by now, wouldn't they? They'd probably be very reassured to hear the details from you.'

'Michael doesn't have parents,' Lee said with harsh brevity. 'Not ones that are of any use to him, anyway.'

'Oh. . . Then. . .?'

'He lives in a squat. So does Mark. They've essentially been on their own for four years—since they were twelve and fourteen.'

'Oh, no. . .'

'Not the only ones, unfortunately, but two who are going to be OK—largely thanks to the Camberton Youth Arts League.'

'Are they brothers, then?'

'Step-brothers. And of the four biological parents they once had between them, one is dead, one in prison serving a life-sentence, one a hopeless addict, and the other abandoned the two of them with a rather violent relative and disappeared off the face of the earth. They're very good for each other.'

'Except when one shoots the other in the chest with an arrow while they're horsing around. . .?'

His snort acknowledged the truth of this, then he added

seriously, 'Mark will never forgive himself for it. As the elder, taking responsibility for Michael has done a lot for both of them.'

'Where's Mark now?'

'Gone home with Glenda Thorpe, another one of our committee people. I'm sure he wants to see Michael, but not tonight. In fact, I doubt if Michael would be out of Recovery yet so I might stop and eat somewhere. Would you. . .?'

Like to join me? He left the question unfinished. She wanted to say yes. . .perhaps too much. The attraction she felt for him surged once again, stronger than ever. Michael's accident this afternoon had cut through the mood of easy intimacy threaded with undercurrents of awareness, but now here it all was back again as if they'd spent the whole day alone together. Wasn't that the best reason in the world to say no?

But Lee took the decision out of her hands, stopping outside a little corner kebab house and telling her with authority, 'Unless you've got something else on. . .I'd like your company.'

'I'd like yours, too, Lee,' Karen admitted.

They didn't spend long over the meal. Didn't talk much, either. Somehow it wasn't necessary, and Karen didn't want to hear herself prattling on with the sole purpose of trying to cover up something that *couldn't* be covered. Lee wanted her, and she was beginning to know that she wanted him.

It was there in the caressing timbre of his laughter, and in the way he licked the tart yoghurt kebab dressing from his finger. It was there in her own quickened breathing and in her awareness of his trousered legs, carelessly brushing her own bare ones beneath the small table every now and then.

When they finished it seemed natural to ask if she could come to the hospital with him to see Michael, and he nodded easily as if he'd been expecting the question.

The sixteen-year-old was in Intensive Care, lost amid the usual shockingly impersonal array of tubing, dressings and monitors. He was conscious and recognised Lee at once but was too drowsy, from his prolonged general anaesthesia and strong pain-killing drugs, to do more than smile weakly and rest one hand limply in Lee's supportive grip.

'So, what do we call you from now on, mate? Robin Hood? No, I guess he wasn't known for being on the receiving end, was he? Mark's with Mrs Thorpe for the night. What nasty medieval thing should we do to him, eh? The rack? The cat-o'-nine-tails? No, seriously, he's punishing himself enough over this; badly wanted to see you but we said no. Tomorrow, OK?'

There was a faint, groggy sound from Michael.

'Can I give him a good report, meantime?'

Another nod and a smile.

Lee then brought Karen forward and praised her skills at splinting embedded arrows in a ridiculously exaggerated manner before stopping suddenly to add, 'Oops! Bet it hurts to laugh. Sorry!' A few minutes later they left, knowing that Michael needed rest more than anything now that he'd had some reassurance. . .albeit of a backhanded kind.

'You were somewhat merciless,' Karen suggested as they crossed the dark and now-chilly car park.

'What, with my talk of Robin Hood and medieval devices of torture? Karen, can you imagine what response any sort of sentiment gets from these lads?' he demanded roughly. 'They distrust it intensely. They've been given words of love and care before, and it's come to nothing. All they trust is action. . .and humour.'

'Do they remind you of yourself and your brother?' she asked suddenly, remembering the sparse but revealing comments he'd made about his family on Monday when she'd had dinner at his house. Was it really only five days ago? In emotional terms it seemed a lot longer.

'Very much, actually,' was Lee's quiet reply. He glanced sharply at her. They were driving now and she couldn't help watching him at the wheel, although she could see little of his face in the darkness. Shadows from the streetlights chased over it at intervals, illuminating the strong, intelligent shape of his forehead, the tired hollows which had now shadowed themselves beneath his long-lashed eyes and the compassionate bow of his mouth.

He was silent for quite a long moment after those last words, then he began to talk—about Mark and Michael, and about himself and his brother, Alan. Karen heard of the latter's delinquency, Lee's difficult decision at twenty to take fifteen-year-old Alan to live with him and the tough love that had been needed to get the younger brother back on track. Alan was in the army now, and doing well.

They reached Karen's flat and he pulled up outside, then they both continued to talk because this seemed far more natural than to cut off the conversation with goodnights and thanks. It was nice, cocooned like this, his shoulder just inches from her arm as he draped himself comfortably in his seat.

Fifteen minutes later, though, the idiocy of the whole situation struck her and she said on a laugh, 'Would you like to come in for coffee? I should have asked straight away. It's not as if we're teenagers, trying to avoid a chaperoning parent.'

'Teenagers?' he drawled. 'Hardly! But. . . *Is* there a chaperone?'

'N-no, there isn't.' His meaning was unmistakable, as was the golden fire in his gaze. She blurted foolishly, 'But I don't. . .want to stay up too late.'

'Then I won't keep you up too late,' he promised lightly. He pressed his fingertips against her lips for a moment, as if to seal the promise, and the gesture was as potent as a kiss.

Once upstairs, she told him to put on music. 'The choice isn't great. . .I have ten compact discs!'

So perhaps it wasn't so very significant that she knew in advance exactly which one he would choose. Yes, here were the first notes of music now—the slow, sensual tones of the singer, Sade. Karen's hand trembled a little as she stood in the kitchen, and she spilled some grains of the rich coffee she was spooning into her little two-cup espresso pot. The dark aroma of coffee in her nostrils only added to the atmosphere.

Making a pretence of activity, she clattered coffee-cups, spoons and milk jug with deliberate vigour—needing to postpone the moment when she joined him in her tiny sitting-room beneath the umbrella of Sade's smoky voice.

He must have grown impatient, however. Or perhaps her fuss over the coffee-making was irritatingly transparent. Whatever the case, the espresso pot was just beginning to bubble and hiss thickly when a sound in the doorway startled her and she turned around to find him there, filling it with his strong frame—the palms of his hands pressed taut against the jamb. Automatically she balled her hand into a fist against her chest as she gasped.

'Karen?'

He lunged towards her, and suddenly there wasn't any point in pretending any more. Her arms were reaching towards him when he enfolded her, and her mouth was opened to receive his kiss. A groan vibrated from his chest as their lips met and she felt his shuddering against her breasts, making them pulse with awareness and desire.

His hands burned over her body, cupping her jaw so that he could drink the taste of her and then searing down

to her thighs to stroke upwards against the tender flesh—
nudging the swell of her buttocks beneath the loose cuffs
of her shorts. Almost at once she felt the hardened rod
of his arousal nudging at her hips and knew that the twin
points of her nipples had become taut in a betrayal of
need that was just as strong as his.

He groaned again, a primal sound that struck a vibrant
harmony within her like a tuning fork. She splayed her
fingers to run them through the feather satin of his hair,
then found the sinuous curve of his nape and the smooth
bracket of his jaw.

'Oh, Karen. . .'

'Lee.'

'You don't know. . .'

'I do. . .I do!'

She had never felt like this before. She'd had tentative
dates in her early twenties with men who were little more
than boys and then there had been Paul, who had touched
her need to give but had never shown her what it could
be like to receive. . .

She stretched her head back, arching, so that her throat
was open and her breasts both invited his touch and
begged for it and he gave her this at once, brushing his
fingers lightly across the aching buds then cupping her
in his palms before grasping her hips and pressing his
mouth against the gap in her blouse where a button had
come unfastened to show the lacy edge of her bra.

The coffee began to burn. Karen couldn't understand
what the smell was at first that impinged on her over-
loaded senses. Then Lee pulled her with him to the stove,
his mouth still moving hungrily against her, until he
reached the knob, switched it off and grabbed the
espresso pot to move it to a cooler spot. The black plastic
handle had overheated and he hissed and swore mildly
as it burnt his hand, but as she began to exclaim he shook
his head and dragged her away again.

'It's nothing. . .and I don't want coffee now, anyway. Do you?'

'No. . .'

'All I want is. . .' His kiss completed the statement. 'I've been wanting it all day, all week. God! Seeing you there having your fortune told, my heart gave a leap—'

'It didn't show.'

'How about now?' He took her hand and pressed it against his chest. 'Can't you feel it?'

And she thought that she could sense the hammering. . .or was that only her own pulse?

'Why are we standing here?' he muttered and, before she knew what was happening, he'd scooped her into his arms.

'Wh—?'

'The couch. Since I intend to do this for hours. . .'

And this was when she came to her senses. No, that wasn't the right expression. Her senses relinquished their total control over her being.

'Lee, I— This is wrong,' she told him, her voice not nearly as firm as she wanted it to be.

'*Wrong*?' He stiffened instantly, and she felt the change in him all along the length that was pressed against her.

'Yes.' Still far from even in tone.

'How could it possibly be wrong?' he demanded roughly, and she flinched until his voice deepened and became a caress once again. 'Just to kiss, alone together, when we're both uncommitted elsewh—' She stared down—her vision a blur—and he rasped, cutting himself off. 'But you're *not*, are you? You're not free! There's someone else.'

'I— Yes.' She was tempted to qualify the statement, embroider it with details and doubts and maybes, but there was something so starkly simple and direct about the way he had put it that it seemed cowardly and pitiful to try and soften the situation.

'The man at the hospital,' Lee was saying. 'Paul. . .'

'Yes.'

'You're not engaged to him, are you? God forbid, *married*?'

He was gripping her shoulders, his hands hard and large and warm, and they were still standing far too close. Just an inch or two closer and her breasts would graze his chest, and if she could bear to look up at him she would almost be able to nudge that strong jaw with her nose or bury her face in the smooth curve of his neck.

'N-no, nothing like that.'

'Then what? What's the situation? Tell me, so I can understand how a man you never mention, a man no one at Linwood seems to know about—because, believe me, if anyone on staff had been discussing ''Karen's boyfriend'' or had caught a glimpse of the two of you together I'd have heard about it—can have such a claim on you that you're prepared to deny. . .*this*!'

His lips seared hers once again, then travelled to her neck, generating such heat and awareness that she shivered convulsively.

'God knows,' he went on in low tones, 'I hope I'm possessed of enough honour to let a woman go when she's committed elsewhere, but. . . What's his claim on you, Karen?'

'Don't! Don't!' She was fighting him off now, fighting off her own desire for him—as they both recognised.

'I *will*,' he seethed, 'until you *tell* me!'

'I—I can't. I—' She hugged her arms around herself to bring a measure of control. 'It's a mess,' she said finally, 'and I don't know yet what's going to happen. You're my boss, essentially, and—'

'Your boss!' he erupted. 'My God! Is that really important? I like to think that at Linwood we're not enslaved by the sort of corporate mentality that tries to forbid the growth of normal human relationships between people. If that's how you see me, as your boss—someone on the other side of the fence whom you can't trust enough to be honest with—then perhaps—'

'No, it's not. Of course it's not!' she beseeched him. 'And yet—'

'And yet,' he echoed harshly, 'despite the chemistry that's exploded between us over the past week, coming on top of something that was already good—a friendship, and a good working relationship—you don't trust me enough to tell me about your connection with this Paul, who somehow makes *us* impossible.'

'No, I don't,' she admitted in a low voice. 'I don't trust you to understand or forgive the madness that came over me—'

But there was no point in continuing. He had turned from her angrily, his breathing tight and harsh and his strong shoulders stiff, and was already on his way out the door.

'Lee?'

He turned, his dark eyes blazing with golden sparks. 'Yes?'

'Forgive me for. . .for letting it get as far as this. I— I should have been stronger.'

'No,' he said heavily. 'Perhaps *I* should have been.'

And, with that enigmatic regret, he was gone.

CHAPTER SEVEN

'No CHARLOTTE today, Pete, so where are we going to put you?' Karen said to the sixteen-year-old as she wheeled him into the dining-room for Monday's lunch.

She looked around the noisy room. Since he was new to the area, Pete wouldn't be starting his special school programme until September but the other teens and pre-teens in residence at Linwood at the moment were all away at their day schools—apart from one profoundly retarded and wheelchair-bound fourteen-year-old who had a bladder infection and needed even more special care than usual.

Hamish's condition was a degenerative one, and after this stay at Linwood he would probably only survive for a few more months at home. His inevitable death, while tragic, would come as a relief from intolerable pressure for the rest of his family. Meanwhile. . . Karen watched Staff Nurse Diane Bristow, struggling to feed him. . . It would be no kindness to Pete to place him in the vacant spot at Hamish's side.

She saw Ross North at the end of another long table, still alone and looking very grim, and on an impulse she wheeled Pete over, ignored Ross's glare and parked Pete beside him—to receive the merest nod of greeting.

'I'll be redoing your pressure-sore dressing straight after lunch,' she told the other man. 'Meet you in your room, shall I?'

'Sure,' he answered heavily. 'Be sure to catch me before I head off to do a little painting with my teeth.'

'Fine. I will,' she said, although it was clear from his tone that he had no intention at all of fronting up at the art and craft room. His relentless cynicism angered her, and must surely have angered Pete, too—Pete, who would give a lot to be able to hold an instrument steadily in his teeth and paint or write or use a computer keyboard.

Controlling herself with difficulty, she turned her shoulder deliberately to the quadriplegic and began to feed Pete his soup. Their eyes met and the sixteen-year-old laughed, a nuanced sound that reflected the complexity of what he was feeling.

'You're pretty terrific, Pete,' Karen told him.

He raised his eyes to say, 'Yes!'

Over Karen's shoulder there was a studied silence. Ross had his soup in front of him, as well as the special spoon and hand attachment that enable him to feed himself. He wasn't touching his food, however.

'Jill puts down a drop-cloth at home,' he said belligerently to Karen, 'and uses plastic tablecloths. As if I was a toddler. Or a vegetable, like that one you're feeding there.'

Unprofessional to turn away from him? Now she wanted to take the man and shake him by the shoulders.

'Pete is *not*—' She would not say the word in front of the boy. And if Ross had been aware of anyone but himself these past six days, he would have known this. 'Pete—' who was laughing again '—is a highly intelligent sixteen-year-old who happened to be born with cerebral palsy. He can't feed himself because he doesn't have the motor control. In fact, even chewing and swallowing can be difficult. But with the help of his sister at home he's half-way through writing a play and he's already finished a collection of poems. Haven't you, Pete?'

Turning to the teenager, she found that his expressive eyes were signalling to her frantically—focusing down and to the left. She saw the little satchel wedged beside him in the wheelchair and guessed aloud, 'You've got a copy of the poem book there?'

He raised his eyes.

'And you want Ross to look at it?'

Again, his eyes went up.

'There you go, Ross,' she told the other man lightly. 'Something for you to do this afternoon instead of painting with your teeth, since you seem to find that idea so distasteful.'

She took the typed and hand-bound booklet from the satchel. 'This one?'

Again Pete signalled, 'Yes.'

Ross North was brick-red as Karen tucked the booklet into the chair beside his thigh. 'Sorry, mate, I didn't know, OK? I just assumed. . .I'm really sorry.'

Pete gave the uncontrolled shoulder movement that meant everything a shrug can mean.

'Is he. . .?' Ross asked tentatively.

'I think he's telling you not to worry about it,' Karen said, and Pete's eyes moved upwards once again.

She went back to feeding the teenager and at once saw that Ross had manoeuvred his spoon into his bowl. He finished soup, bread and custard tart without another word, then growled reluctantly as the meal came to an end, 'Perhaps Jill's right about the drop-cloth. I suppose there's no sense in having to get the dining-room carpet shampooed every two weeks.'

'Practicality before pride?' Karen suggested carefully. 'People seem to find it *gives* them more pride in the long run.'

'Yeah, well. . .' He stared down broodingly once again at the rain of soup droplets and pastry littered around him on the table and floor.

They met up again half an hour later when Karen had completed a small post-lunch drug round and co-ordinated the afternoon's plans with the rest of the nursing and therapy staff. Ross's pressure sore had improved in the six days he had been at Linwood, and both he and the nursing staff were taking care that no further danger areas developed, but there was still some work to do on this one before it fully healed.

After removing the old dressing and cleaning the area, Karen left Ross to sit in front of an infrared lamp for some minutes in order to increase circulation and dry out the ulcer. She then put his leg through a range of passive movements, which would also stimulate circulation and promote healing. Antibiotic powder and a fresh dressing completed the procedure.

'There! That looks good,' Karen said as she refastened Ross's clothing.

'And no good asking me how it *feels* because that's the whole point, isn't it? I *can't* feel it,' Ross said, with a little less of the black cynicism he usually showed.

'Exactly,' Karen told him. 'And you might be interested to know that one of our day patient's wives, Dorothy Makepeace, spotted a danger zone on her husband's upper thigh before it developed into anything serious, thanks to some of your tips at our session the other day.'

'Yeah, meanwhile my bladder isn't emptying all the way, and I've got another infection—according to Sister Thingummy who was on last night. So it's back on the antibiotics.'

'It's not always such hard work,' Karen told him quietly. 'It's only just over a year since you came out of rehab. Things that still seem such an effort to you will eventually get to be second nature, and when that happens they'll take up much less time and effort.'

'Yeah, like *you'd* know!'

'From seeing others get to that point,' she said, then added with spirit, 'Yes, OK, it's inadequate to spout these things when I haven't been through it myself, but the medical profession could hardly be made up only of pregnant midwives, diabetic gland specialists and cardiologists with pacemakers, now could it?'

Unwillingly he laughed, then sobered at once to say thrustingly, 'Jill's going to leave me, you know. Couldn't stick it out.'

'Well, why should she when *you're* not sticking it out yourself?' she retorted bluntly.

'Not sticking—!' He was furious, and she hoped that this was a good thing—to get it all out, like lancing an infected wound. 'How the hell am I not sticking it out? I'm stuck in this body, aren't I, for the rest of my days?'

'Yes, but you're as emotionally absent from your body, and from your marriage, as if you'd packed a suitcase and caught a train, and it seems to me that *that's* what Jill can't stick. Why should she? It's not your quadriplegia she can't stick—it's your reaction to it. I don't blame her! And in this case you *can't* tell me I haven't been through it myself because I have!

'And I made the decision you're afraid Jill's going to make. I couldn't stick it. But it was the man, not the illness. He tried to use the illness as a way of accusing me of cowardice but he was wrong, just as you're wrong about Jill—and if you don't see that then you'll lose her.'

She stopped abruptly, knowing that—according to any guidelines about nursing—she had said way too much, but sensing in the sizzling anger of the man in the wheelchair opposite a healthier response than any he had given yet since his arrival at Linwood.

Then she sensed something else. A figure in the doorway. Lee Shadwell, immaculate in a navy suit, white shirt and scarlet and grey silk tie. He looked stunning dressed this way, and it distanced him from the far less forbidding uniformed Lee who could cheerfully put up a drip, change a dressing or even give a sponge-bath.

'I haven't got more than a minute, Karen,' he said tersely.

'You need to see me?'

'I do now. . .'

He withdrew from the doorway and she followed him quickly, aware of her body's heat rising as she nervously brushed down the skirt of her dark blue uniform. He had a meeting this afternoon at the architectural firm that was drawing up the plans for Linwood's Stage Two development, but this wasn't about that. She expected him to go to his office but, instead, he pulled her abruptly into the two-bed room next to Ross North's, unoccupied at the moment as its patients were involved in daytime activities.

It was less than two days since their explosive late-night encounter at her flat and this was the first time that she had seen him since then. He'd been involved in administration all day, she guessed—closeted in his office on the phone or at the computer, or wading his way through the piles of papers that no one in management ever seemed to get done with these days.

She had known that their parting on Saturday had been as awkward for him as it had been for her; wondered if he had dwelt on it as she had and hated the fact that Paul was mixed up in it too. She had arrived at a groping understanding that although by rights she should have felt that Lee's kiss had compromised what she owed to Paul it was, in fact, the other way around, and she wished desperately that she could have been fully free to take Lee's offered sensuality without the unfinished business of her past tangling her feelings.

Now. . .

'What was that about?' Lee faced her angrily, kicking the door shut behind him as he spoke.

'I—' There was something powerful and very sensual about his anger moulded into every line of his body, and it was all she could do to stop herself from swaying into his arms to beg for his understanding.

'Telling a patient that his wife is going to leave him, and that you fully sympathise with the woman because it's what you did yourself!'

'It wasn't—'

'It was, Karen. I heard it.'

'OK, but in this case—'

'And it was not only unprofessional,' he ploughed on inexorably, his voice not raised but steely and quiet which was far worse, 'but I have to ask myself, not for the first time, why it is that you're not prepared to discuss this man, Paul—it *was* Paul that you meant, wasn't it—with me at all when you can happily sketch out the very essence of your relationship with him to a near-stranger who is, furthermore, a patient?'

'Lee. . .' She hadn't known that those golden glints in his eyes could look so steely.

'I have to wonder, after what you said the other night about my status as your boss, whether you feel there's some conflict of interest or something at stake that compromises your role here at Linwood.'

She was miserably silent for a long moment after this icy tirade drew to a close. The wild thought throbbed inside as she groped for words, It's what I've been afraid of all along—that Paul would jeopardise my job, and now he has and it's almost *because* I tried to keep silent about him. How. . .how very mythic and Greek! If it was just my job, though—if I was having this blow-up with some budget-obsessed management type—I'd scarcely mind. It's the fact that it's Lee, and he's probably right. I *did* go overboard with Ross North. . .

'Look, I'm late already.' Lee's voice cut in on the downward spiral of her thoughts.

'I'm sorry, Lee,' she managed. 'I'll try and repair the damage with Ross. And if. . .I mean, please ask for any details about Paul and I'll tell you. Perhaps I've been wrong to say nothing, and if you think it's grounds for me to leave Linwood then I'll hand in my resignation as soon as you like.'

'Oh, hell!' He slammed a fist into his palm. 'We've got to that, have we? And we can't talk about it now because I really *cannot* be later than I already am!'

He seized the door and was through it again in a minute before she'd managed to speak at all. In any case, she knew that anything she could get out at the moment would only sound inane, if not worse, in the face of Lee's pressing need to be at his meeting. She sighed and echoed his profanity under her breath. 'Oh, hell!'

It didn't help.

And then, opening before her as a rent in the clouds might open to reveal shafting sunlight, came the knowledge, I *can't* go back to Paul. It's what I said to Ross North. It's not the illness, it's the man. And Paul himself would be the last man in the world to respect me for doing what goes by the name of 'duty'. He'd laugh himself silly at such an outmoded idea.

Lee wouldn't. Lee believed in duty. He'd said so in no uncertain terms to Jill North last week and, being outside her situation with Paul, he would in all likelihood never understand.

It was bitingly significant that what she had half-knowingly feared all along should have happened in this way. Through Paul she had lost Lee's good opinion, and only now did she realise quite how vital it had become to her.

'Hey!'

She had got herself into the corridor some seconds after the churning wake of Lee's angry departure had subsided, and had almost forgotten what she was doing in this part of the building when Ross North hailed her impatiently.

'Yes, Ross? Are you planning to head off to the recreation room now?'

'No, I'm not,' he growled. She thought, Oh, no, he's reached the same decision as Lee—that I was horribly out of line in saying what I did. But then he went on, still belligerent, 'If you must know, I want to sit and read these poems of Pete Larkins! If it's permissible, of course!'

'That's fine, Ross. Of course it is.'

'Yeah, well, can you get me some kind of book bracket, then, because you known damn well I can't hold something like this *and* read *and* turn the pages at the same time!'

She got the special attachment to the wheelchair that he needed and fixed it in place, still wary of his mood and what it would mean. He said very little, and she wondered if it was the calm before the storm.

But when he did speak finally his hesitant tone suggested that he was almost as surprised by the contents of his speech as she was. 'Thanks for what you said earlier. About Jill and me, and your own experience. I . . . appreciate that you let down the barriers a bit.'

'That's. . . Well, it did come out rather more bluntly than I'd intended.'

'I'm pretty blunt myself,' Ross North told her. 'As you may have noticed. And I don't promise. . .I mean, I don't believe in bloody miracles but I'll try while I'm here. . .as along as you *tell* Jill that I'm trying, OK?'

'OK.'

'Now, did. . .? You see, I couldn't help overhearing a bit next door. Tone and volume, not words. Shadwell was angry, wasn't he?'

'Er. . .yes.'

'I'll let him know that you didn't crush my darling little ego, or whatever it was.'

'No, please. It's all right. It was. . .a management issue, actually.'

'Hmm. Was it? OK. Still. . .'

'Don't say anything to him, Ross.'

The man grimaced in a noncommittal way, and she had no idea whether he'd take any notice of her request. She left him reading Pete's simple quirky poems.

Later that afternoon, just before her scheduled departure time, Karen caught up with Mary Thomas in the craft room to promise, 'I *will* fit in your self-cath lesson! If you'll just give me until after report. Fifteen minutes, OK?'

'Fine. I'm still attempting to resuscitate this rather crummy little pinch pot, anyway.'

'Put a handle on it and call it a milk jug?' Karen suggested.

Mary laughed. 'Perfect! Then I can pretend that this kink is its pouring lip.'

The milk jug was finished when Karen returned so they started out at once for Mrs Thomas's room, matching their speeds so that Karen was at Mary's side.

'Nice to be able to talk,' the older woman said. 'I never feel I can when people insist on walking behind to keep out of my way. Although if there was a way to bring me up to normal standing height. . . There isn't, I suppose. My wheels would be five feet high!'

Just then they both became aware that there was a little commotion taking place in the corridor beyond the foyer. Mrs Tostell, tight-lipped and querulous in her wheelchair, was complaining loudly to Staff Nurse Bristow.

'I *did* tell you! Twice!'

'Yes, and I'm sorry I wasn't able to attend to you at once, Mrs Tostell, but when I did finish with Mrs

Masterton and Mrs Potts you said it didn't matter any more.'

'Because I'd already *been*.'

'But you didn't tell me that.' Diane Bristow was keeping her patience with difficulty. 'And it was an hour ago.'

'Well, my daughter should be here now. She'll look after it all when I get home.'

'Oh, please let's not have you going home like that, all wet, Mrs Tostell. . .'

'Is there a problem with my mother?' Judith Grey said as she entered the building. 'It's not her ankle again, is it?' Mrs Tostell's hairline fracture was still firmly bandaged.

Diane turned to greet the elderly woman's daughter and explained that Mrs Tostell wasn't quite ready yet as she needed to change her clothes.

'Oh, dear, again?' was Judith Grey's resigned reply.

'Perhaps we should look at continence pads—at least until her ankle is healed,' Diane suggested as Karen and Mary Thomas passed on beyond them.

Mary suppressed a sigh and Karen knew that she was facing the issue of her own inevitable deterioration of continence. She said a minute later, as they neared her room, 'Is there any point to this, Sister Graham? Perfecting this self-cath technique, I mean. It's not easy, and. . . Perhaps I should just give up now.'

'You certainly should not,' Karen told her briskly. 'You've told me that you don't even need catheterisation normally, and that you have excellent bladder control using the Credé manoeuvre when you're on the toilet.'

This was the simple use of hand pressure on the lower abdomen at the level of the top of the full bladder, triggering it to empty. 'Now, during this exacerbation it makes sense to perfect a different technique. And ten years down the track, sure, you might need something else, but having a range of options is the key. Don't give up! Get control!'

'Thanks,' Mrs Thomas said on a wobbly laugh. 'I usually give myself that same pep talk, but it's nice to have someone else do it for a change. You're right, of course. I normally deal with it all very well, I think. . .'

'You do.'

'But every now and then. . .'

'Everyone has chinks in their armour.'

They went through the self-cath procedure carefully together. As Mary was still new to the technique she needed a mirror for guidance, and found the longer catheters that men used easier to hold.

'Still nervous, I'm afraid,' she said. 'Even after the two sessions we had on this last week. That short one for women looks impossible to me!'

'You'll get it,' Karen promised. 'And it'll fit into your purse, it's cheap and it lasts quite a while. Now, first let's put the jelly on the catheter tip. When you buy it for yourself do make sure it's this water-soluble kind, not petroleum jelly.'

Mary took the catheter and found the small opening of her urethra, then successfully inserted the lubricated tip. 'Now I can relax, can't I? It just slides from here and. . .'

'Terrific!' Karen told her once the bladder was fully drained. 'I think you're ready to do it on your own next time.'

'Um. . .'

'Try?'

'If you really think so!'

Karen spent a few more minutes going over the cleaning of the catheter and answering a couple more questions from Mary, then packed up her equipment ready to put away. She heard Lee's voice in conversation with Alison Parker and realised as she said a quick goodbye to Mary,

He's back from his meeting, and I was hoping he wouldn't be. I really don't need to see him again today!

She was going up to the hospital now to see Paul for the very last time, and it wasn't an encounter she could look forward to—which was why she knew that she had to do it straight away and why she *didn't* need a further scene with Lee, or even a mere frosty greeting if they crossed paths in the foyer.

How is Paul going to react? she thought. Just how badly will I hurt him. . .no, not *him*, his ego?

But, although perhaps the ego of a man like Paul was not the most fragile part of his psyche, she still hated what she had to do because this time she truly knew that it was final and a failure of sorts for both of them, despite all she had learned about herself and about life.

Thinking all this as she picked up her bag and light spring coat from the staffroom, she had forgotten about Lee and practically cannoned into him on her way out of the door. For a telling moment they were pressed length to length and she felt the crush of her breasts against his chest and the bracketed strength of his hips in their tailored trousers, thrusting against her stomach.

'Lee! Sorry. . .'

'My fault. I was hoping you hadn't gone.'

'I should have,' she retorted absently. 'I'm twenty minutes late.'

'As usual.' The words were gently spoken, and suddenly there was the light caressing of fingertips along her jaw and she subsided, flustered, back into the room as he clearly wanted her to do. 'Karen, I won't keep you. . .'

'It doesn't matter.'

'But I need to apologise for earlier. Ross North talked to me just now and says that, unorthodox or not, what you said to him helped.'

'You're right, though, Lee, I probably shouldn't have said it. It. . .it was too personal.'

'Listen.' He moved closer. '*I* was too personal. *My* reaction. I was angry because you hadn't talked about that stuff to *me*.'

'I—I know, and I will, Lee, if you feel it's affecting my work.'

He gave a hiss of exasperation. 'Damn it, Karen! It's not your work and you know it.'

His kiss engulfed her mouth before she could draw breath so that her gasp of surprise was stifled by the onslaught of his lips. He held her upper arms in a masterful grip that drew her close enough to squeeze her breasts against him. Her arching response was instinctive and all her own doing, and the feel of his mouth on hers was so compelling that she was almost lost within the moment at once.

'Lee. . .'

'Tell me to stop. Tell me to stop if you owe this man Paul something! You must because *I* can't. I don't know his claim. You haven't told me so *you* must be the one to stop, Karen!'

He was daring her, challenging her, demanding that she tell him, 'No, Paul has no claim. I don't owe him anything that's stronger than this kiss,' but she couldn't do it because all his impassioned words served to do was to bring into stark focus the fact that Paul *did* have a claim—in her own mind, at least. He had one right remaining, and that was the right to be told first of her decision—to be told before she told Lee.

And, perhaps even more important, she knew that she owed this to herself as well. She could not give herself to Lee—verbally, physically, emotionally—before she had done what she needed to do to make herself free.

'Then. . .then stop, Lee!' she gasped at last, the effort almost overwhelming. 'I'm telling you— Stop!'

He did, his face drawn into stark lines of disbelief and distance as he pulled away. 'You mean it, don't you?'

'I—I have to.'

They stared at each other, eyes glittering and faces flushed.

'I've been wrong, then.'

'Bad timing, Lee?' she suggested desperately.

'Just that?'

'I—I don't know.'

And there was the strong sense between them, communicated in the stiffening of bodies that had been melting together just moments ago, that neither of them ever would know. Timing? Fate? A brief, mistaken fling?

'Go, then, would you?' he suggested lightly. 'While I collect myself. Because I imagine I'm not going to have long in which to do it.'

At that moment they both heard Alison Parker calling, 'Lee?' and knocking at the door of his office just across the corridor.

'Of course. I. . .need to get up to the hospital anyway or I'll clash with the patients' dinners.'

The humour didn't come off and her mention of the hospital was too contentious now, giving form to the shadow of Paul that lurked between them—as it had done all along.

'See you tomorrow,' was such a meaningless phrase under the circumstances that neither of them bothered to utter it and, a scant half-minute late, Karen was hurrying, half stumbling, down the driveway to catch the Number 17 Camberton Hospital bus which was already approaching its stop.

I think. . .I *know* I could have loved him, came the feverish, miserable thought. It doesn't seem possible now. He said he'd been wrong. Wrong in thinking he wanted me? Hardly surprising when it must seem to him that I've been stringing him along or stringing Paul along.

Both of them! If I'd told Lee the whole story straight away....

But she was back to square one with that idea. She hadn't told him because she'd been afraid even then—before she suspected her own attraction to him—of earning his disapproval. The situation was a thing of her own making, and all she could do was face the fact.

With a grinding of its engine, the hospital bus pulled up in front of her.

Paul Chambers was in a very bad mood. Staff Nurse Julie Wilson, just two hours into her late afternoon shift, warned Karen of the fact as she passed the nurses' station.

'I've already had one junior in tears.' There was a slightly accusing note in her voice and Karen flushed, aware once again of the prurient disapproval some staff at the hospital betrayed on the subject of her relationship with the older journalist.

She was under no illusion that this would change once it was clear that she was no longer involved with him. At some level—by people like Julie Wilson—she would be branded for ever. Branded. It wasn't a pleasant word and, when she thought inevitably of Lee, she decided, At least I've avoided having him know the details!

Gritting her teeth, she donned the breathing mask that she hated so much and entered Paul's room. On Saturday, at around this time, he had been asleep. Today he was wide awake, sitting up in bed with one of the books she had bought for him.

And scowling.

'Hi,' he growled as soon as he saw her.

The restless displeasure in his blue eyes set her to explaining uncomfortably at once, 'It's been a few days, I know. I did come on Saturday, but you were asleep and—'

'Did they tell you I'm still not responding to the antibiotics?' he interrupted harshly, seeming uninterested in her excuse.

'No. . .' And the news tore at her. Whatever she might feel about Paul now, she did not want this!

'So I guess they didn't tell you I'm leaving, either?'

'*Leaving*? But Paul, you—'

'I'm going back to the US—under medical escort, which rather tickles my fancy. Obviously I need more aggressive treatment than this third-rate country can provide, and I'm sure it'll be available in New York. Turns out that if we fudge things a bit I'm still covered by Lynette's health insurance, hot-shot lawyer that she is.'

'Health ins—! *Lynette?*' With her painful decision about their future uppermost in her mind, she couldn't grasp his words at all.

He shifted a little awkwardly. 'Ah. . .hmm. I. . . imagine I've failed to mention Lynette in the past.' Now he grinned, like a little boy caught in some piece of mischief that, surely, wasn't so *very* naughty? Then the scowl was back on his face. Was it anger at his disease? That didn't feel quite right. . . 'My second wife,' he explained now. 'We're not actually divorced, and so—'

Karen went cold all over, her attention fully focused now. She said woodenly, after a telling moment of silence, 'You always told me you didn't believe in marriage.'

He gave a snort of harsh laughter. 'Quite! Because I've *been* married—twice! Still, Lynette seems to feel— we talked for an hour on the phone the other day—that there still may be some life left in the old mare if she's flogged a bit. . .Whatever! It's the health insurance that's the real concern.'

'I hope she agrees with you on that.'

'She's a bit more of a cold-blooded realist than you'll ever be, my dear little Karen, and apparently she has reasons of her own for wanting to rekindle our relationship.' His blue eyes were glittering wickedly in his once-handsome, leonine face, and his smile was utterly arrogant. 'You're angry?' he demanded suddenly, and the scowl returned to his features. Could it possibly be. . . guilt, about Karen herself?

'Yes, you're well rid of me, aren't you?' he growled. Then he had another chameleon-like change of mood. 'But, be honest, didn't I give you the three most exciting months of your life? Our little place in Tangiers, right in the centre of it all? Talking about writing and ideas? Incredible sex. . .?'

But Karen had gone, ripping the respirator from her face for the last time. Oddly, she *didn't* feel angry any more. Not guilty, either, about what she had been planning to tell him. The score was even between them now.

In fact, most people would probably consider that Paul has won far more than he's lost, she realised as she left the ward, oblivious to the scrutiny of the staff. And that I've been the biggest loser all round. But I refuse to look at it that way! I've learnt some hard lessons from this and it's not the way I would have chosen to learn them, but perhaps it was the only way. I'm not going to let this eat at me, and drag me down. And I mustn't think that it could have been different with Lee if I'd known. I can only try to put it behind me and go forward.

Meanwhile, Paul Chambers would be gone, and Karen sincerely hoped that the American doctors he was now pinning his faith on did have some medical miracles awaiting him, all nicely covered by his wife's health insurance.

CHAPTER EIGHT

'WELL, of course, in those days we had them at home, a lot of us, didn't we?' Wheelchair-bound Adeline Webb looked around at the small group gathered in one corner of the patients' lounge at Linwood, her eyes bright with memory.

The reminiscence session had started informally during this Friday's afternoon tea between a group of the elderly patients currently in residence. The day patients had gone now and Karen felt that she really ought to be getting on with other things but Lee had slipped her a note, telling her that she should stay and ask questions to keep the flow going.

He believed strongly in the connection between emotional and physical healing, and with the past such a powerful presence in many old people's lives. . . As usual, Karen found that she agreed with him on this point almost instinctively.

Mrs Webb went on, 'Which was nice for some and not so nice for others. And, of course, most of us didn't have a clue what was going on unless we were lucky and had someone to ask, like an older sister who'd been through it and wasn't too prim. It was traded like precious currency—any information you got—wasn't it, girls? How much does it hurt? What does the midwife *do*?'

Mrs Masterton giggled comfortably and so did Miss Stroud and Mrs Ruppert, although the latter's words were unintelligible as ever. It was probably a new experience for them to be talking about childbirth so frankly with men present, but popular Adeline Webb was very bold of speech and opinion, and had got them all going.

Harry Makepeace, who was staying late today, said, 'Course, us blokes didn't get a look in. Both of ours— my wife's pains started during the day, and I went off to the shop; put in a day's work. Just came home to find my sons and went out again to the pub to celebrate. Got drunk as a skunk! No idea of what actually went on.'

'You forget that yourself, anyway, as soon as it's over,' Mrs Webb said.

'One forgets too much. Far too much,' Honoria Masterton added. 'I had only one child, my daughter, and then she had children of her own and used to ring me up and ask me, "Mother, what did you do about nappy rash?" or, "Mother, did I have colic?" and for the life of me. . . So much of it was just gone. It's as if, when she grew up, she got in the way of all my memories of her as a child. I—I can't remember what it was like to love her then.

'My daughter's back tomorrow, and I go home!' Honoria Masterton's cheeks were an excited pink now. 'I'll see a lot of her, too, because there'll be lots for her to do. It'll take her a good week to get everything straight in the house, so I'll see her nearly every day. It'd all be *far* too much for me to do on my own at my age.'

'So why don't you move to a smaller place, then?' Harry Makepeace asked bluntly, then muttered. 'Rich bitch,' very rudely under his breath. Fortunately Mrs Masterton didn't hear.

'Oh. I. . . Well. . .' She brushed her neat blue skirt over her knees with flustered hands. She glanced at Mr Makepeace and then looked away. 'What would Lucy do in a smaller place? There'd be no need for her to come and—' She broke off, fidgeting uncomfortably. 'It's my home, after all. I belong there. I have a right!'

There was a change in the atmosphere. Things had become uncomfortable. Karen felt it and evidently the others did too. There was a shifting in seats and a clearing of throats. Mrs Masterton repeated in a high voice, 'It's my home. And I have a right to my own daughter's help. I've brought her up to know her duty. She might not come if—' Once again the sentence remained unfinished.

Mrs Webb whispered to Karen that she needed the toilet. Two more patients, who had only listened to the more vocal participants, started talking to each other while Mrs Ruppert listened in, nodding and giving the garbled twitterings that were her speech now. Like Mrs Masterton, she was going home tomorrow but, after some persuasion, Mr Ruppert had seen that day hospital would be best from now on as his own surgery had left him frailer than before and in need of extra rest.

Mrs Masterton, on the other hand. . .

What a resilient, stubborn old thing she is! Karen thought. Somehow she doesn't think she can claim her daughter's time out of love, so she appeals to her sense of duty. That's why there's all the fuss about the big house and its need for maintenance and housework.

'Think I've worked out the hidden agenda with Mrs Masterton and that big house of hers,' she told Alison Parker twenty minutes later as she prepared to leave. The deputy nursing manager, who finished at nine that night, would be back on duty tomorrow morning when Lucy Masterton Stevens was due to collect her mother and settle her in at home.

Alison chuckled at the idea of buying time with the demands of housework. 'Devious old thing, and yet I don't think it's quite as deliberate as that.'

'No, it's not,' Karen agreed. 'One of those little games we all play with our own emotions and feelings. We pretend we don't know what we're really doing. If Mrs Stevens can come up with some good ways to spend lots of time with her mother that *don't* involve considerable amounts of physical labour. . .'

'And I'm sure she will because I get the impression she's very fond of her old mum.'

'I imagine dear Madame Honoria would be much happier in a small, sunny flat.'

'Yes, her place must be horribly lonely and dark in the winter.'

'What was that I heard just now about little games with our feelings?' Lee wanted to know, sticking his head around the door of the office where the two women stood.

'Oh, we're being very profound on the subject of human nature, aren't we, Karen?' Sister Parker said.

'Well, we certainly have a fair bit of it to study here at Linwood,' Lee drawled and they all laughed, though Karen's sounded rather false to her own ears and she was very aware of how impossible she now found it to meet his gaze.

It was five days since Monday's scene with Lee and her last revealing visit to Paul, and it was like the aftermath of a storm in many ways. All that turbulence, her feelings buffeted here and there like a fallen branch blown by the wind, but now. . .now. . .a calm of sorts was returning. The kind of hushed, frozen state where you don't quite dare to breathe in case something is broken.

There was a fraught awareness on her side, a stiffening in her limbs when he got within range—the same sort of way the tiny hairs on one's skin stood on end in a sudden chill. As for him. . .

'You look tired,' he told her bluntly after the laughter had died away.

'Call it Friday-itis,' she quipped lightly.

'I'll call it anything you like if you promise me you'll get home and pamper yourself for the rest of the day.'

Could Alison detect the sub-text there?

Lee knows I haven't been sleeping well this week and that it's due to him. Apparently he hasn't had the same problem. What a fool I am! He's already managed to put it all down to what might have been, while I. . .

'Hot chocolate, a nourishing meal and a soak in a warm, scented bath,' Lee was prescribing with authority.

'Yes, sir!' teased Alison.

He turned to the other woman. 'You're right! It *is* an order!'

'Are you going to knuckle under to that kind of out-rageous dictatorship, Karen?' Alison said.

'Actually. . .I think I am.'

And she was stretched out in her steaming tub within the hour, her bathroom billowing with a steam redolent of frangipani bath oil and quiet music seeping through the door from her FM radio in the other room. Scented baths and soft music notwithstanding, though, it hadn't been an easy week.

'OK, so eight units of fast-acting,' said Staff Nurse Diane Bristow.

'Eight units fast-acting insulin,' Karen confirmed, drawing up the dose for the elderly blind man, Mr Thompson, who was one of their regular day patients.

It was almost lunchtime, and this was the last patient on this particular medication round. Karen swabbed today's site on his left thigh and gave the injection. He smiled and nodded when it was over.

'Good technique for someone who's not diabetic!' He made this same joke every day.

'Well, I'm getting so I've had almost as much practice as you,' Karen teased in reply. It was a response she knew he liked.

With many disabilities now—some related to age and others very directly to poor control of his diabetes in years past—Mr Thompson could no longer manage his own injections, and his erratic appetite made it hard to keep his blood sugar within the normal range. Karen had tested it half an hour ago and timed his pre-lunch insulin dose accordingly. Now it was up to him to eat!

'Fish today, Mr Thompson,' she told him.

'I like a nice piece of fish,' he nodded, smiling with his sightless eyes closed.

'What's going on in Lee's office?' Diane Bristow murmured as soon as they left the activities room where their patient had been doing some craft-work.

'Don't know,' Karen answered with a shrug.

'There've been tears and traumas in there for the past ten minutes. Aren't you curious?'

'I will be. . .when I've got this drug trolley checked and put away, and the cabinet safely locked!'

'Well, *I* am!'

'Is that why you tried to double Mrs Ellis's dose of thyroid medicine?'

It was a mild reproof, but a reproof nonetheless. With two nurses always called upon to do each drug round, the systems were well in place to avoid errors but no one could afford to be slack or distracted.

Diane fidgeted and turned down her mouth. 'I caught it as soon as you did. I wouldn't really have given her the wrong amount. And, admit it, a crisis in Lee's office. . .'

'I'm sure he's handling it.'

'Oh, I'm sure he is, too. But it's Mr and Mrs North, isn't it? Ross is supposed to be going home on Monday. His three weeks will be up, and we hadn't heard a peep from Mrs until today.'

'Is it? The Norths? Both of them?' Karen looked up sharply from the trolley she was pushing.

'Aha! Got you now, haven't I? You're as curious as I am!'

Karen suppressed a sigh. She didn't really like Diane, and certainly didn't like her way of expressing things. Yes, she was *very* curious now. Ross had been trying so hard over the past ten days and his wife's failure to get in touch with him had been ominous, although he had said nothing. But Diane's attitude made curiosity seem like a frivolous and rather cold-blooded emotion.

Staff Nurse Bristow was looking back towards Lee's office now, with the same avid regard she might have shown if she was standing outside Buckingham Palace hoping for a glimpse of one of the royals in tears.

Karen went so far as to say, 'Well, I hope Lee's able to help them find the right solution.'

And Diane took this as sufficient encouragement to suggest, 'Maybe we could pretend we forgot Mrs Appleton in her room and dawdle past?'

'Diane, we have forty-five patients to get seated in the dining-room within the next ten minutes!'

The other nurse shrugged. 'OK. We might never know now. And I'd love to see our Lee presiding over a happy ending. I bet he'd do it beautifully. Although I guess *you're* not a romantic.'

'I wouldn't say that!' Karen was stung to the retort.

She regretted it a moment later when Diane cajoled, 'Go on. Let's put this away as fast as we can then you can pretend you've got something to ask him, and I'll hang around in the corridor.'

'Why me? It's your idea! You do the pretending.' She was half amused, half irritated. Diane had the tenacity of a dog worrying at a bone when it came to certain things. When it came to others, however, she was decidedly slack!

They reached the supply room at the far end of the corridor, where the drug-trolley was stored and the drugs themselves locked securely away. Diane had already begun ticking off their list in a rapid, absent sort of way but now she stopped, dropped pen and paper with a clatter and a rustle onto the trolley and looked up at her senior with her green eyes narrowed in sudden spite.

'Bloody hell, don't pretend you don't know! You've

got him wrapped around your little finger. I saw you strolling around the stalls together at that medieval fair of his two weeks ago, and since then he's alternated between eating you up with his eyes and staring at the floor every time you enter the room.'

'Diane—'

'And you,' she ploughed on relentlessly, tossing her head. 'I can't make you out at all. If you're *not* interested—and evidently you're not, because if you are you've got a funny way of showing it—then leave the field clear for me, and stop those blue eyes of yours from doing their one-picture-is-worth-a-thousand-words act whenever you see him. If it's one thing I can't stand it's a tragedy queen!'

She whirled around and seized the door, pulling it open with her blunt hands.

'Stop! Wait!' Karen cried.

Diane's words had frozen her at first, but now she was desperate to correct the morass of wrong assumptions... even though some of what Diane had said was far too perceptive for a girl who could hardly remember her patients' names at times.

'Wait?' The staff nurse echoed derisively. 'What for? I want to suss out that scene with the Norths for myself, if you won't, before it's over and done with! Judging by your attitude to Lee, you've obviously got a *major* problem with indecision!'

She was gone in a moment, her dark curls bouncing, leaving Karen to lean shakily on the metal drug trolley. It was all jealous, frustrated nonsense, wasn't it? If *she* hadn't managed to put her thwarted response to Lee behind her, as she had so badly needed to do, then *he* certainly had. Diane's observations might be sharp, but they were way out of date.

Paul must be gone now. She hadn't heard from him—hadn't expected or wanted to. And Lee had been achingly formal and polite on the few occasions when they'd been alone together. If he managed a bit of their old banter when others were present, it was only for show.

Burningly self-conscious, although she was entirely alone, Karen hugged shaky arms around herself, chafing at the plain dark blue cotton of her uniform. Her breasts tingled and she relived each of Lee's kisses with an aching sense of loss and awareness of what might have been.

Then, with a determined firmness, she picked up the pen that Diane had dropped and checked off the list of drugs and patients, putting the unused medicines safely in their designated place in the drug cupboard.

Nothing was missing. Nothing was in greater quantity than it should be. Nothing that needed immediate restocking, since a separate check each week generated an order-list for Lee to deal with. She locked the cabinet and held the cold metal key tightly in her palm. It should be returned to Lee's office immediately. . .

Wheeling the trolley into its corner, she left the supply room, locked its door also and walked on cotton-wool legs down the corridor. She briefly registered that Diane, clearly unhappy at the fact, had been waylaid by a patient but then was hardly aware of the hubbub of patients' conversation as they gathered in the dining-room and the savoury smells of poached haddock, chips and vegetables which wafted through the doorway.

What she *was* aware of was the door of Lee's office opening suddenly as she approached it, and Mr and Mrs North emerging. The latter's face was tear-stained and the former's grimly determined, but Jill North's hands were on her husband's shoulders in a caress as he pushed ahead of her in his wheelchair and both had the aura of hope and tentative renewal hovering around them.

Immediately behind them was Lee himself, looking quietly satisfied. 'There's a long way to go, but with the start you've made today. . .' he said.

'We'll get there,' Jill replied, and it was like the renewal of a vow. 'Won't we, Ross?'

They disappeared along the corridor, not having noticed Karen at all.

Lee caught sight of her, though. 'Drug cupboard key?'

'Yes.'

'I'll put it away.' He took the scrap of metal, now warmed from her over-heated palm, and she was aware in her new, painful way of the touch of his fingers against her own. Her pulses beat faster and she deplored the self-consciousness which made it almost impossible for her to look at his satisfied face.

'There's been a breakthrough, I gather?' she made herself say cheerfully, staring at his capable chest which was rising and falling with steady rhythm—although her own breathing was hard to control

'Yes, the essential first step which is that they've both made the commitment to go on trying.'

'What happened? What changed for them?'

'Come in and I'll tell you.'

She summoned a light tone. 'I should warn you that Diane Bristow is keen to hear the details of a perfect romantic reconciliation.'

Lee made a face. 'If it was that, I'd worry. When people promise each other the moon and stars they often don't think there's any more work to do. In this case. . .'

'Something must have changed, though.'

'Jill had a break and had a chance to consider her priorities. And as for Ross. . .a combination of Mary Thomas's example, the other people he's met up with here and, as he phrased it, "that damned kid's poems".'

'Pete Larkins.'

'Yes. There's one he wants photocopied so he can put it on his fridge. At eye level, he said. I've given them a list of books which I hope he'll find encouraging and inspiring but not too sugar-coated, as well as the names of a couple of counsellors.'

'That's good, Lee. Although Diane might be disappointed. She seems to think that people's feelings are not acceptable unless they're cut and dried.'

He gave her a sharp look, detecting the undercurrent of personal meaning, but didn't comment. Instead, after a short silence, he said,

'Lunch rush on?'

'Yes, it is so I better go,' she said brightly.

'Before you do. . .'

'Yes, Lee?' Her breathing was suddenly shallower than it should have been, and the words came out in a high, thin tone that sounded very unnatural to her own ears.

'I thought you might be interested to hear that Michael's coming out of hospital today.'

'Already! That was quick!'

'Yes, he did extraordinarily well. In fact, his doctors did want to keep him in for a little longer but any kind of institutional setting, no matter how benign, has such bad connotations for him that they were convinced to discharge him early on condition that he get professional attention at home every day for the next couple of weeks.'

'"Were convinced", Lee?' she accused gently. 'By you?'

'Well, yes. . .'

'And I expect you're providing the "professional attention", too!'

'I detect a lecture about my workload in the wind. Save your breath. Alison's already given it to me. But—'

'You can't let Mark and Michael down?'

'No, I can't,' he admitted quietly.

'How about sharing the load, then?' she suggested on impulse, feeling a surge of concern and care for him that could not be dampened by the awkwardness between them of late. 'Take me round there one day, show me the routine and then let me alternate with you—if they'll have me.'

'Are you serious?'

'Of course. I wouldn't say it if I wasn't prepared to follow through. Are you. . .so surprised that I'm willing to forego my spare time?' Have I lost your good opinion so completely?

He looked at her sharply, as if she'd spoken this last question aloud. 'Of course not. Except. . .I rather thought you were still committed to visiting your friend. . .*Paul* in hospital.'

'Paul's gone,' she told him briefly, hating the sound of the other man's name. 'To the United States, for further treatment there. It's. . .unlikely that he'll be back.'

There! She'd been trying to find a way to tell him this, as her misguided reticence had nagged at her and left a sense of incompleteness.

'Is that. . .? Look, it's none of my business but is it a problem for you that he's gone?'

'No, it's not. Not now.'

A tense silence stretched between them. None of his business. Well, if he felt that way then it wasn't. . . Although she longed to say to him, It *is* your business if you want it to be. It would have been your business if I'd recognised the fact earlier. The timing was wrong, that's all.

'If you're really interested in helping out with Michael's dressings. . .'

'I am,' she made herself say, although she felt exposed and vulnerable with the words.

'Not this week, perhaps. They're like dogs who've had a cruel master. Slow to trust. How about if I bring you over a week from tomorrow, when Michael's improved and I've talked to them about you coming.'

'Whatever you think best, Lee.'

'Right now I think it best that we both help get the patients settled for lunch.'

She laughed and nodded, thinking, Maybe it's possible that with enough time we'll have an easy friendship again. I'm going to miss it badly if we don't.

An uneventful week followed. Ross North left—to pick up his life at home with renewed commitment to his marriage and the management of his disability. Mary Thomas had gone, too, still in the grip of her multiple sclerosis exacerbation but eager to see her husband and sons again after their trip away. Mrs Masterton's daughter rang to thank the Linwood staff for their insight into the old woman's excessive demands for help at home, and Pete Larkins sent Lee a copy of the first act of his play.

'I'm going to show it to Melody,' Lee said, 'because it's terrific and she's looking for a new, large-cast, kid-orientated piece for next year. This just might fit the bill.'

And Mr Makepeace and Mrs Tostell were still with them as day patients, of course. The latter was becoming increasingly difficult to deal with. There had been several problems growing out of her ankle fracture and consequent lessened mobility, including swelling in her legs and 'dizzy attacks' when she changed position—caused by low blood pressure.

'We'll all be relieved when that ankle is pronounced fit!' Lee spoke for all of them. 'Hopefully, on Monday!'

Meanwhile, Mark and Michael had given their OK to Karen accompanying Lee to their squat on Saturday afternoon, and though she reminded herself that it was in no sense a 'date' Karen couldn't help looking forward to it more than she should.

He. . .*nourishes* me, even now when we're so careful with each other.

* * *

The day dawned with all the sunny promise of June in the air. Karen was dithery on the phone to Susie, arranging to see a film together one night the following week, and this didn't do a lot for keeping her feet on the ground.

Then she let the washing-machine flood the laundry at the back of her block of flats when she forgot to check that the drainage hose was properly positioned in the wash-trough. Fifteen minutes of mopping up followed. . . And then she almost did it again when washing her sheets and towels.

Her sandals were soaked now—the ones she had planned to wear this afternoon—and another tenant of the flats had appeared three times at the laundry door, looking very peeved at having to wait—not to mention having to negotiate a wet cement floor.

A lunch of fresh bread, salad and a tangy piece of Cheddar seemed to stick in her throat, despite the three large cups of tea she drank to wash it down. . . And then all that tea turned out not to have been such a good idea because it made her as jittery as strong coffee since she wasn't used to so much at once.

'Why didn't I just chase the whole lot down with a stiff whisky and really mess myself up?' she said to her reflection in the mirror at three when she decided that it was time to get ready.

Then that reflection caught at her skittering thoughts and she studied it, dissatisfied with what she saw. She touched her fingers to her slightly parted lips and remembered Lee's kisses once again. Pretty lips, yes, and pretty hair, a petite, curvy, quite passable figure and eyes that reflected her new uncertainty as she tried without success to quantify her assets as if she were a racehorse or a vintage car. Lee had been attracted to her. To the outward image? Or to something he thought he saw beneath? And what did he see now?

Pointless questions! All this attempted analysis was only making her feel worse.

Turning to her wardrobe, she faced an equally difficult task. What did one wear to a squat? Flats or heels? Dress or shorts? Jewellery and make-up. . . Running shoes?

Abandoning that line of questioning, she then asked herself what she wanted to wear for Lee. And again drew a blank. Safe, chaste, dull? Or the opposite? She remembered Melody Piper's get-up at the fair, and posed for a moment before the mirror in her lacy cream underwear like a page-three model.

'That's right,' she told the mirror sarcastically. 'High heels, skimpy shorts and a push-up bra. Just the thing!'

Finally she collapsed onto the bed in frustration, and decided that she was really falling apart!

But when Lee arrived at a quarter to four she was ready—just—in a floral print sundress, a light brush of make-up, a thin gold chain around her neck and last year's sandals—which looked better than she had feared.

He seemed to approve. . .and yet the atmosphere between them was decidedly tense at first. It was her fault because words just wouldn't come.

Lee said only, 'I'll be interested in your reaction to the place.'

'I'm curious. . .and a bit sceptical that Michael was discharged here straight from hospital,' she admitted.

'I had to take the hospital social worker on a tour. *She* was extremely impressed!'

It was a fifteen-minute journey, ending with a winding driveway which led to a sizeable old house standing all by itself—almost concealed by overgrown trees in all directions. Since Karen had been expecting an inner-city tenement she was further intrigued, and the crippling self-consciousness she had been feeling with Lee began to slip away.

There was a rather meek-looking 'No Trespassing'

sign and a very new-looking 'For Sale' sign, both staked
in the ground about ten metres from the house. Lee
steered the car between these to pull up by the front steps
where two old bicycles were propped, both equipped
with large, sturdy carriers at the back.

The yard—you couldn't call it a garden—was a wil-
derness of weeds and junk, and Karen could see that two
of the front windows were jagged with broken glass that
had been roughly patched with now-yellowed newspaper.
So far she wasn't impressed, and wondered a little at the
social worker's reaction.

Then the front door opened and small, wiry Mark stood
there, looking younger than his eighteen years. He gave
a quick salute to Lee and nodded at Karen, held the
creaking door open for them and ushered them inside.

The place was awful! Shattered bits of plaster and
broken brick littered the front hall and obscene, crudely
painted graffiti adorned the walls. Through another door
she glimpsed a big old fireplace filled with ash and rusted
cans, though oddly the surrounds of the fireplace were
carefully covered in newspaper and tape.

It was a complete shambles. . .although, even as she
thought this, Karen was struck by the impression that
there seemed to be something curiously *theatrical* about
it all. She saw that Lee was studying her with one corner
of his mouth lifted and his eyes definitely twinkling.
She shrugged slightly and he smiled more widely, his
gold-flecked eyes fixed on her until they brought a blush
to her face.

'I think you've added some more touches since I was
last here,' he said to Mark, turning away after a moment.

'Yes, the graffiti's brill, isn't it?' was the casual reply.
'Violent as I could make it. Washable paint, of course.'

'But I see the place is for sale.'

'Yes.' He was leading them up the central staircase.
Karen went last, too aware of the way Lee's body moved

ahead of her. 'The legal bull over the estate is all done with at last.'

'Problem for you, then?' Lee was saying to Mark.

'Actually. . .' Mark looked somewhat sheepish '. . .the lawyers are handling another contested estate. Similar situation, like. They've asked us to be caretakers until it gets sorted out. Could take as long as three years, they say.'

Lee gave a shout of satisfied laughter, while Karen was thinking, *Caretakers?*

The teenager still looked a bit sheepish as he went on, 'We didn't think they knew we was here, but turns out they did. Must have snooped around one day and decided we was looking after the place, like, so they didn't get the police in.' He clearly had a twinge of doubt about this explanation, and Karen noticed that Lee was saying nothing.

Then Mark threw open a door which led from the wide landing at the top of the stairs and suddenly, as they entered a spacious passageway, the impression of vandalism and dereliction was totally gone.

Michael lay on a mattress in a large bedroom, through the windows of which summer sun poured like a golden curtain. Although sparsely furnished, it was immaculately clean—even to the crystal teardrops of the ornate antique light fitting overhead.

There were even some decorative touches—a bunch of dried grasses stacked in a clean, white enamel jug and two water-colour prints, which were so pretty that you almost didn't notice the stains of age and damp in their corners and the inexpertly mended frames. Two kerosene lamps, unlit at this hour, sat on the marble mantelpiece above the fireplace where flames leaped brightly beneath an old kettle.

At the sight of Lee and Karen, Michael struggled to sit up, greetings were exchanged and Karen was reintroduced to the injured teenager as he had been too groggy from anaesthesia that night three weeks ago to remember her visiting him in Intensive Care.

'I've moved the kitchen in here till he's doing better,' Mark said to Karen, gesturing, and she saw the neatly arranged things beside the fireplace—a couple of sauce-pans, plates, cups and cutlery and an oddly assorted 'pantry' which included four badly dented cans of soup and stew, a sparse collection of tired vegetables and several eggs so fresh that they hadn't even been washed yet.

'Speaking of doing better,' Lee said, accepting a spot at the foot of Michael's mattress, 'when do you next go back to the doctor?'

In a courtesy that she recognised immediately, Mark ushered her to the one chair—a terrible old thing in green vinyl dating from about 1972. Again, though, despite erratic springs, uneven legs and tears in the vinyl, it was perfectly clean and she sat down on it without a second glance.

'S'posed to go Monday,' Michael was saying.

'Supposed to go, and you will,' Lee retorted. 'Mean-while, let's have a look at your gory wound.'

'It isn't even very gory any more,' Michael answered, sounding quite disappointed.

Lee put on sterile gloves from the pack of equipment he had brought, carefully removed the dressing and checked the wound for inflammation and drainage. Karen stayed where she was, not wanting to seem too pushy today. She could see, though, that the area was healing nicely. Lee cleared it and applied antiseptic, before creating a new dressing—lighter than the old one and permitting greater freedom of movement.

'No inflammation,' he pronounced. 'This dressing has to last till the doctor on Monday. Then if it's OK with you blokes I'll send Karen to check on you Tuesday and Wednesday.'

'OK,' Michael shrugged gruffly.

Next Lee listened to his chest and heart, took his temperature and pulse, just to make sure, and asked a few more questions about how Michael was feeling.

'Still hurts a bit,' was the laconic summary. 'But it's better every day.'

'Good lad! Don't let the dressing get ratty.'

'He won't. Don't worry!' Mark growled. 'I'll see to it.'

'Yeah, like you saw to it in the first place with your brilliant aim,' Michael retorted.

'Good way of keeping you out of trouble, I've decided. I'll do it again if I have to, I will, to keep you in line.' Mark added an extremely insulting epithet, but Karen was no longer fooled by appearances on this odd occasion. The two stepbrothers were completely loyal to each other.

'Hot-cakes should be ready, shouldn't they?' Michael suggested now.

'Oops, yeah, they should,' Mark nodded. 'I'll get them out of the oven and make the tea.'

'Hot-cakes?' Lee queried, as Mark used a piece of bent wire to pull an old, lidded cast-iron pot, evidently their oven, from the fire.

'It's what we call 'em,' the eighteen-year-old was saying. 'Just made them up. Flour and water, or milk and an egg if we have them. Nice when they're still warm, and with jam or honey when we have that. Today, luxury of luxuries, we got both, we have, and butter as well.'

'Mmm, they're a kind of scone, and absolutely delicious,' Karen said five minutes later when presented with her tea in a cracked mug and her 'hot-cakes' and jam on an old glued-together saucer, which was Minton china—if she wasn't mistaken.

'Scones? Fair enough. We just make stuff up from

what we've got and give it names,' Mark said.

'Hungerarian ghoul-ash,' Michael supplied.

'That's when supplies are low and we're pretty hungry. We put in everything we've got, mixed up together.'

'And Spanish omelmix is eggs with anything what takes our fancy.'

'Carrots didn't work too well, did they, Mike? They didn't cook.'

'You two need a recipe book,' Lee suggested.

'Yeah, but we'd never have all the ingredients at once.'

'I hope you're getting paid for the caretaker job?'

'We are, and there'll be the electricity on and water and everything.'

'If you'd like me to look it over for you—make sure the conditions of employment are OK and it's all above board...'

'Don't worry!' Mark scowled. 'We know when we're being ripped off. It'll mean Mike can go back to school, that's the main thing.'

'Yeah, but I don't—' Michael began.

'You're staying at school, you!'

'And what about you, Mark?' Lee asked.

'Nah! He's going to be the brain. I'm going to keep on with this stuff. Caretaking, maybe gardening, renovating places myself one day. This new job'll make me legit if we do it well, and I'm going to do it *bloody* well! I'll be able to get references.'

'The Youth Arts League will give you one.'

'I'll take it!' He added, 'Tell Melody, though, I might not have too much time for building the *Romeo and Juliet* set now.'

'We'll manage.'

Karen said little during all this, content to marvel at it all—the boys themselves and their self-sufficiency, pride and determination, masked by the frequently rough manners and this place, a real home, kept deliberately hidden behind the façade of dereliction.

Perhaps most of all, though, Lee and his acceptance of them—the way he made sure that everything really was 'OK' without putting them off with lectures, instructions or too much interference. He seemed truly at ease, squatting in front of the fire to pour more tea—his strong body moving fluidly as he rose again.

'Would you like to see the rest?' Mark asked Karen some time later after tea and 'hot-cakes' were finished.

'I'd love to!' she exclaimed, meaning it. She was quite curious, for example, about those fresh-laid eggs.

Lee flashed her an approving grin and the three of them set off, after Mark had gruffly ordered Michael to go to sleep. The next room along was Mark's bedroom and opposite, across the corridor, was 'the study'. Karen was surprised at first. . .and then, once again, impressed. There were Michael's school things, an odd assortment of battered old books on all sorts of subjects—acquired from goodness knew where—and some diagrams and notes on scrap paper that Mark casually dismissed as 'just ideas'.

Then there was a bathroom containing toothbrushes, towels and several buckets of water but little else, and she thought, Of course, no running water. . .I wonder where they do get it from.

Down the back stairs was the big old kitchen where Mark normally cooked on another open fire. There was an old electric range, too, but without power it was useless, of course. And then a clucking sound solved the mystery of the eggs—two hens, who divided their time between the old scullery which had been fitted up as their abode and a crudely fenced area of yard where food scraps provided their pickings.

A pipe which ran from the roof gutters into a big clean plastic barrel solved the mystery of the water supply, and Mark said offhandedly, 'If you need the loo, Karen, there's an outhouse just there. We move it round, see. Just dug a new pit yesterday, so it's fresh.'

But she felt that this was one experience of squat life that she could manage to miss.

'We should get going,' Lee said. His fingers trailed lightly across Karen's forearm as he addressed her, his eyebrows raised. She nodded, and felt the fine hairs on her arms stand on end at his touch.

'Yeah, and I want to do my supermarket run,' Mark answered. 'Running a bit low. The bins out the back of the shops on Grace Road are usually pretty good on Saturdays. Unsold stock they can't hold over till Monday.'

'Just make sure it's not contaminated,' Lee warned gently.

Mark grinned. 'I've got pretty expert and pretty picky these days.'

'Shall we say goodbye to Mike?'

'No.' Much more serious now. 'He'll be asleep. He wasn't too comfortable last night, and he still gets pretty tired.'

'Don't let him miss the doctor on Monday.'

'Course I bloody won't!'

At the car, after Mark had gone back in, Karen took a last look around at the horribly overgrown front yard, the blind windows of the apparently derelict house and the sun—dazzling and dappling through the breeze-swayed trees. 'Incredible!' she said.

Lee laughed. 'It is, isn't it?'

As they drove she asked him, 'Aren't the social services involved at all, though? Isn't there somewhere they could go?'

'They don't want to. It's been tried time and time again and every time they've run away and found themselves a squat—most nothing like this—and been found weeks later, having industriously created a clean and tidy home for themselves. Finally, a perceptive case worker realised that this was how they were happiest and left them to it.

'Naomi Barker. She's good. She didn't want them to drop totally out of sight, though, so she sent them along to us with strict instructions to get them heavily involved in anything that Mark would perceive as useful in expanding his self-sufficiency and survival skills—carpentry and that sort of thing. That worked. . .or else they were starved of social contact with other kids. . .and, much to our relief and surprise, they've stayed.'

'It also seems incredible that they *didn't* get evicted from here, despite it being obvious that they're not destructive.'

'Ah, well. . . As to that. . .' He hesitated, his well-moulded lips tucked in at one corner.

'Your doing?' she guessed, having suspected it before.

'Don't ever tell them!'

'*Would* I?'

'Sorry. . .' His glance flicked briefly away. 'Yes, I went along to the legal firm that's been handling the estate and the contested will. Had to make quite a sales pitch but convinced them in the end that these two would keep any real vandals or far more destructive squatters at bay.'

'Convinced them? Just like that?' she probed.

'Well, no,' he admitted, again with some reluctance. 'I had to take legal responsibility for any damage they caused.'

'Lee, if they'd burnt the place down, or. . . You could have lost your parents' farmhouse!'

He shrugged. 'It was an act of faith. You have to make them sometimes. It's paid off.'

'The caretaker job?'

'Yes, and that's something I didn't have a hand in, which I'm glad about. Mark's less naïve than he once was, and I'd hate him to suspect too much fiddling behind the scenes.'

'Naïve? Kids like that?'

'In an odd way, yes. About the way organisations work; the relationship between individuals and institutions.'

'Yet so streetwise and cynical in other ways.'

'So mature and self-reliant,' he added lightly, 'and yet capable of horsing around so stupidly that one of them shoots the other in the chest with a bow and arrow. Kids are like that.'

'They are, aren't they?' she said. 'And not just kids.'

They were back amongst the streets of Camberton by this time and she saw that he was taking her straight home. Well, what had she expected? Outside her flats he didn't switch off the engine but sat there at the wheel, just watching her steadily and smiling a little while she fumbled over the words of her thanks and appreciation so that again, to her own ears at least, it didn't sound sincere.

'Thought you'd find it interesting,' was all he said as she finally stumbled to a halt, and her attention caught on the word.

'Far more than just interesting, Lee! Very life-affirming, somehow.' She was aware of the colour that came and went on her cheeks, and not so aware of the fact that she was now leaning eagerly towards him. 'Those two are such an example of the . . .I know this sounds silly. . .resilience of the human spirit!'

'Doesn't sound silly at all,' he told her gently. 'And I happen to agree with you. A dose of Mark and Michael in their native habitat always has me coming away with the belief that anything is possible.'

His smile caught at her and made her heart turn over. Oh, what a weird feeling it was, too! Like a frog doing a backflip in her chest. She swallowed. . .her throat was tight. . .and she wanted him to kiss her so badly that her full lower lip trembled and she had to catch at it with her teeth. It wasn't going to happen. . .

He wasn't smiling any more. The engine was still running and he was staring ahead now, frowning as he drummed a tattoo on the steering-wheel with his lean fingers.

'I—I must go,' she managed.

'And you're sure you want to go back there on Tuesday and Wednesday?'

'Quite sure, and the route's pretty simple to follow. Susie's already said I can borrow her car.'

'Great! I appreciate the fact that you wanted to stay involved. Meanwhile. . .'

'Yes,' she agreed quickly, 'I'll see you on Monday.'

Alone in her flat a minute later, she thought miserably, How did this happen? How did he get to matter so much after just two months of friendship and that night when we kissed?

He was so different from Paul! *He* had deliberately set out to manipulate, capture and possess her, whereas with Lee. . .

I've done this on my own, she realised. And that's the only way I'll get out of it. On my own.

Over the following nights she slept very badly.

CHAPTER NINE

DURING Monday morning's report from the night staff a week later, Diane Bristow commented on Karen's fatigued appearance. 'Your eyes look like two holes burnt in a blanket.'

'They feel like it, too,' she managed to retort cheerfully.

Since it was true, there was no point in resenting Diane's words, although Night Sister Roberta Adams spoke up on her behalf, saying mildly, 'You know, Diane, it is possible to make that sort of observation in a more tactful way. You could ask her if she had a bad night and offer to make her a cup of tea, for example.'

But Diane only answered sourly, 'She's already got coffee.'

'That's not the point I was trying to make.'

Diane shrugged, still miffed. 'Well, perhaps you can—'

Maggie Allan interrupted, rather crotchety herself after a long night shift, 'Let's get on with the business at hand, shall we? Unless you lot *like* having everyone late in to breakfast and your whole morning a mad rush because of gab-festing in here. Personally, I'm ready to go home.'

A late June heatwave was brewing after over a week of glorious weather, and even at this hour there was a heaviness in the air today. Some of the elderly patients liked the increased humidity, saying that it made their joints looser, while others complained of 'a nagging pain' in left shoulder or right knee or in the wrist they had broken seventy years ago as a child.

'Nagging pain?' Diane was heard to mutter during

155

breakfast. 'The whole day is going to be a nagging pain if you ask me!'

Things were a rush. Maggie's prediction was certainly accurate there. An excursion had been arranged for this morning to Camberthorpe Castle. It was Lee's doing after the contact he'd made with the new American owners, Vance and Lila King, at the time of the medieval fair, and he would accompany the group. It consisted of a large complement of the adult day and resident patients, necessitating an extra bus in addition to as many staff as could be spared and several volunteers.

In view of the Kings' generosity in opening the place up for the Linwood group, Lee had asked that a special effort at punctuality and smooth organisation be made.

So far, with the humid air heating up by the minute, his request was in danger of going by the board.

'Mrs Tostell is just *determined* to come,' Gaye Wyman hissed at Karen, when they were already assembling the patients in the foyer to wait for the buses.

Accompanying an excursion group wasn't something that the part-time physiotherapist normally did but, like many other people, she'd missed out on the castle's open day at the fair and was eager to see it now so she had volunteered some extra time.

'Oh, she is, is she?' Karen sighed. 'She only just had her ankle pronounced fit on Friday.'

'I know,' Gaye nodded. 'And I'm still giving her physio. No chance of wheelchair access is there?'

'What, in a thirteenth-century castle? That's why we've restricted today's outing to mobile patients.'

'All right,' Gaye muttered, her hands flapping, 'it was a stupid question.'

'You think she should come?'

'Um, she seems. . .really quite beside herself about it. We all know how difficult she can be. But she's practically in tears, not tight-lipped as she usually is when she feels she's being hard done by.'

Karen sighed, wavering, then had to be realistic. 'No, really, it's just too hard at the last minute like this. We'd need an extra volunteer. I'll talk to her,' she decided, 'even though I haven't got time. . .!'

'She's in the patients' lounge, in her hat and gloves.'

'Oh, dear!'

'With her walking-frame propped up in front of her like a weapon. Meanwhile, should I. . .?'

'Start getting the slow ones out to the kerb. The first bus should be—Yes! Here it is! Good for Mac! Always on time.'

'Right you are.'

'Thanks, Gaye.'

Karen hurried off down the corridor but was waylaid by Lee. A moment's self-consciousness at the sight of his tall, capable figure passed at once as there was simply no time during working hours to think of the way he churned her feelings.

'Is this going to be a logistical nightmare?' he asked her with an expressive grimace. 'Are we in way out of our depth?'

'I expect so!' she told him cheerfully. 'The trouble is that *everyone* wanted to come. They've all grown up on the tales of mad Sir Matthew Braneby and the bloodstains on the stairs.'

'Um, I imagine the new owners might have cleaned those up by now,' Lee drawled. 'And, as far as I know, the much-maligned Sir Matt slumbers in a peaceful grave.'

'But you know what I mean. Some of them actually saw him around Camberton before he became a recluse, and Mr Makepeace used to deliver his meat but never got past the tradesman's entrance.'

'Yes, I do know what you mean. Need help getting them on board?'

'Yes, please! I'm off to persuade Mrs Tostell that she's not fit to go. Gaye says she's in tears.'

'Then perhaps she should go,' was his simple answer.

'Oh, Lee, I think. . .'

'She's not the type to turn on the waterworks over nothing.'

'No, she isn't. . .'

'Look, if I can get her daughter by phone now and get her to meet you lot at the castle entrance. . .' He was already heading towards his office to make the call, the rear view of his tailored trousers and pale shirt even more impressive than the front.

Her heart lurched as usual.

'Brilliant!' she managed. And so typical of Lee—to care enough to make it happen and come up with the right idea. 'I wonder why Mrs Tostell didn't suggest it herself.'

'I wasn't here on Thursday and Friday,' the old lady sobbed a few minutes later, answering the question. Karen had forgotten this. Gnarled old hands trembled like nervous birds inside their neat white gloves. 'So I didn't know about the trip to the Castle. I only found out this morning. And I want to see the castle library so badly! I sold my husband's books after he died to Sir Matthew for his collection.

'I needed the money, you see, so terribly. They were valuable books. Donald valued them so much and I sold them. I had to! Surely he would have understood! Judith and John were only small and I had no training to work. The jobs I could get didn't pay enough to support a family. I'd have had to sell the roof over our heads if I hadn't sold the books.'

'But Mrs Tostell, surely the books won't still—'

'Mr King bought the whole contents of the castle,

including the library. It was in the newspaper. I especially took note of that. Mr King probably doesn't know that some of the books used to belong to Donald. They were his pride and joy. . .'

'Was your daughter going straight home after she dropped you here this morning?' Karen interrupted gently.

'I think so. Not that she ever tells me her plans!' The habitual frosty bitterness was back in her tone for a moment.

'Because we're going to try and contact her. If she can meet us there and help you with your frame; sit with you somewhere if your ankle is giving you trouble—'

'She won't be able to. So typical! She'll be going off somewhere. . .'

But Judith Grey was at home and was very pleased to come. Lee ducked into the lounge a moment later with a thumbs-up sign to convey the news and stayed to accompany Mrs Tostell on her painfully slow trip down the corridor and out the front to the bus, while Karen went to brief the group of volunteers—most of them carers from the patients' homes, such as daughters or spouses—about how the morning was to be organised.

'Ten minutes late leaving,' Lee winced to Karen as the two buses were finally ready. 'I'd better tell Diane to ring the Kings. She won't thank me. She's already miffed at being delegated to stay with the non-mobile patients.'

'Yes, well. . .' Karen muttered, feeling a flush creep up her neck.

There had been another nasty scene between herself and the staff nurse on Friday, and she'd had to field accusations that she was planning to seduce Lee in some little-used castle bedroom. She'd been tempted to take the other nurse by the shoulders and retort, 'I would in a minute if I thought he'd respond!'

She hadn't said any such thing, of course. Not that Diane was impressed by her soothing denials.

Now the growing heat of the day suddenly seemed very oppressive, and she couldn't match Lee's easy conversation with the patients seated at the front of the bus. Everything seemed to stick in her throat.

Mac volunteered rather too enthusiastically to try and make up the missing ten minutes on the drive to the castle but, on seeing the glint of challenge in his eye, Karen and Lee quickly damped down the idea.

'Two buses full of frail elderly careering along doing wheelies around every corner? No thanks!' Lee murmured, taking his seat beside her and filling her awareness with his aura of maleness and musk.

So they were late and lost a few minutes more picking up Mrs Tostell's daughter at the castle gate but Vance and Lila King, themselves in their sixties, didn't seem to mind and welcomed the whole party in with a warmth and innate generosity which went a long way towards relaxing the rather apprehensive staff.

'Oh, good! They're human!' Gaye muttered to Karen.

'But all the same, let's not have Miss Teale pick up any priceless ornaments with her shaky fingers,' Lee came in.

'Or let Mrs Pewsey sit down on any fifteenth-century brocade chairs,' said Gaye.

'Er, no,' Karen agreed. 'We should find out straight away about handy bathroom facilities.'

'And seating for those who fall by the wayside,' Lee suggested.

The Kings had already thought of all this, and had even laid on morning tea for the end of the tour in the library. Inside the castle. . .'Now, strictly speaking, Camberthorpe isn't a castle at all—it's a fortified manorhouse,' Mr King told them all in an enthusiastic, carrying voice that even those hardest of hearing could understand.

The day's heat and humidity disappeared and it was pleasantly cool and airy.

They saw the Great Hall, the kitchens, the armoury, several of the bedrooms, the pleasantly modernised morning-, drawing- and dining-rooms...and lastly the library. Several of the frailer patients had not lasted through all this, with the many sets of steps and stairs that had to be negotiated, but Mrs King had been charming in her conspiratorial, 'Let's leave Vance to extol the serious history. I want to have you all put your feet up in the library and tell me if you know more than I do about those legendary bloodstains and Sir Matthew's grisly grandfather!'

Surprisingly, Mrs Tostell was not one of the faint-hearted, and shook off both her daughter's and Lee's suggestions that she go to the library straight away.

'No, I want to see it all!' she said very firmly. 'Mr King is so interesting, and he knows his history surprisingly well for an American. Though he did make an error on the date of the Jacobite Rising. It was seventeen-*fifteen*!'

'Don't strain your ankle, Mother,' Judith Grey pleaded, but Mrs Tostell was immovable...clearly tired, though, when they did reach the library at last.

Still she wouldn't rest and was at Mr King's side, her cheeks—normally pale beneath her pink powder—quite hectic. She waved aside a cup of tea, wouldn't sit down as he politely urged her to and said eagerly, 'This is the room I really wanted to see, Mr King. I believe you have over four hundred books that once belonged to my late husband. May I see if I can recognise some of them?'

Recognising her enthusiasm and catching Lee's tiny nod of approval, he answered generously, 'Please do, my dear lady! And if there's anything you can tell me about them that I might not know, I'd like to hear. I've scarcely begun to investigate the treasures in this room.'

'What a darling man!' Judith murmured, her eyes filling. 'This is so important to her, and yet I never realised. She's never even mentioned Dad's books.'

'Perhaps *because* they're so important,' Lee suggested quietly.

And Karen told Judith Grey, 'From what she was saying to me this morning when she was so upset, she's never had complete confidence that he would have approved of her selling them.'

'You could well be right. I was only six when Dad died—gosh, it's forty-five years ago, now—and I'd forgotten that he was a rare-book collector in his spare time. But, yes, I should remember that. She never does talk about what's really important—just bottles it all up and comes out with those tight-lipped, nasty little asides that make it so hard for me to remember that she's my mother and I love her. I should try to draw her out more. . . Do you want me to go over with her, Sister Graham? She's starting to look so tottery and tired on that frame.'

Karen watched for a moment as Mrs Tostell and Mr King reached the tall shelves in the middle of the long, beautifully proportioned room. 'He's keeping a very careful eye on her,' she noted aloud. 'Look, now he's pulling up a chair for her.'

'And do you think that perhaps she wants him all to herself for the time being?' Lee suggested.

'You're right, of course.'

'So have a cup of tea and some finger sandwiches and cake with the rest of us. I think we've all earned it.'

'It's been a delightful morning,' Mrs Grey said, turning to Lee. 'I'm so glad you rang me and decided she was fit enough to come.'

'I think she'd have hitched a ride on the rear bumper of the bus if he hadn't!' Karen laughed.

Everyone had tea now, served in an assortment of beautiful bone china cups, and the mouth-watering cakes and sandwiches were fast disappearing. Then came an emotional cry from Mrs Tostell, 'Judith! Judy!' and Karen felt a pang of alarm as she saw the old woman clutching her heart. She met Lee's sharp glance and they hurried over, as did Mrs Tostell's daughter.

There were tears again but this heart pain wasn't medical in origin. 'Your father gave me this book when we were first married,' Ida Tostell said, trembling as she held the leather binding. The fine leaves inside fluttered. 'Look, a first edition of Sir Walter Scott's poems. I didn't want to sell it, but Sir Matthew would only take the whole collection and this was already listed on the inventory. I almost. . .hid it, left it out, but of course that sort of dishonesty would have been quite wrong.' Her lips tightened for a moment in a familiar way, then softened again. 'He used to read them to me. He had a beautiful speaking voice. . .'

'There's something inside, Mother; have you noticed?' her daughter pointed out, and again there was a cry of almost painful joy as she opened the book.

'This card! I'd forgotten all about it. He must have used it as a book-mark the last time it was opened.' She silently read the black ink scrawl on the old-fashioned greeting card, her lips moving, then handed it to Judith who read it too and then turned away, clearly very moved.

Mr King had watched the little scene in silence, as had Karen and Lee, and now he said to Mrs Tostell, 'Sweetheart, I've only got one thing to say about all this and that is, I want you to have this book.'

For a second the sun came out in Mrs Tostell's lined and not very pretty old face, but then she sat up very erect, tightened her small mouth and said, 'My goodness, no! It must be worth a lot of money these days!'

'My dear lady, I already have a lot of money,' he answered comfortably. 'I don't need any more, and what I'd need even less would be to know that I was selfishly hanging onto something which would give you so much pleasure.'

'Then. . .then. . .' The sun was back '. . .I would be honoured to accept it from you,' Ida Tostell said.

It was time to start shepherding everyone back to the buses. Gaye and Louise were both looking at their watches surreptitiously and telegraphing the fact with raised eyebrows to Karen and Lee. Mrs Pewsey had nodded off and so had Mr Green. Several of the very elderly people needed the toilet. Some of the younger ones were still embroiled in exciting tales of the castle's reputed ghosts and scandals with Mrs King, who encouraged the most unlikely poltergeist theories with bright eyes and eagerly clapping hands. Few of the patients or volunteers had even been aware of Mrs Tostell's exchange with Mr King.

Judith Grey was still dabbing at her eyes. 'This has been such a wonderful thing to happen!' she said. 'Mother seems so joyless at times that I get far too impatient with her. And her continence problems lately have been getting to me.'

'We hope she'll improve again now she's more mobile,' Lee said. 'Meanwhile, do remind her about doing the Kegel exercise several times a day. It's never too late to start.'

'Or too early!' Judith Grey laughed. 'We'll do them together.'

'And, seriously, the products available for dealing with incontinence have improved so much in recent years. It's a message that needs to be spread more, especially to women who've had children. There *are* solutions!'

'I know, and I'll find them for her,' Mrs Grey said. 'I'm not kidding myself that she'll be all sweetness and light from now, but I really know now how she loves me underneath and what a good mother she is. That card. . .the things Dad said to her. It must have been so hard for her when he died, and she sacrificed so much for the sake of her children. I'm going to take her straight home now, if that's all right, to rest and talk some more if she wants to.'

'Yes, do take her,' Lee agreed. 'This will have exhausted her.'

Outside, after profuse thanks to the Kings, they'd all forgotten how humid and hot it was and the return journey sparked fatigue and ill-temper in many of the patients after the tiring morning. It made the rest of the day long and difficult.

Mrs Pewsey had a bad bout of the postural hypotension which caused dizziness on standing, and fell in the dining-room after lunch before anyone could reach her. Mr Makepeace had heart palpitations, and so many 'nagging pains' asserted themselves that Karen's sympathy and patience threatened to desert her and she was horribly tempted to give a strong dose of aspirin to every patient, whether they needed it or not!

The wheelchair patients and several others not strong or well enough to go to the castle naturally felt left out so they were crotchety as well, and Karen knew by two o'clock that she didn't have a hope of getting away on time. Still, did she wish the excursion hadn't taken place? Did anyone? No! It was unanimously pronounced the most successful trip that anyone could remember.

Writing up a report on it in the nursing office next door to Lee's at five that afternoon—when she had been due to finish an hour before—Karen held her pen over the paper for a moment, wondering whether to take that sort of shortcut in her report-writing which, inevitably, everyone did from time to time, creating a bland account of the morning that would be of no use to anyone.

Then she thought for a moment and suddenly her hand was slipping fluently across the page.

'Reconciliation,' she wrote. 'A more satisfying form

of healing at times than any well-mended ankle or nicely dried-out sore. If only we had more time to promote such opportunities, instead of having them take us by surprise as happened today!'

Then she thought inevitably of her own mother, and all the bitter things that had been said nearly eight months ago. Was their estrangement to be permanent? She had sent that one card upon first reaching Morocco, even while wondering bitterly whether they'd actually care to know that she was all right.

Since then she had often thought of writing or picking up the phone, but then her vividly-etched memory of her mother's face and her words would return and her heart would harden again.

She told me she wanted no more part of my life. . .

She sighed, the report blurred and forgotten before her gaze until she heard a movement behind her and there was Lee.

'Still writing up today?'

'Oh. . .' She laughed guiltily and blinked back some tears. 'I got carried away. . .and started to think about other things.'

'Want to talk about it?' he suggested easily. Those tears hadn't escaped his notice, then.

'I—'

'Don't you think it's time you did, Karen?'

There it was again—that resonance between them, losing the jarring quality it had had lately and becoming pure and simple once again.

Tell him the whole story? At least by this time she had nothing to lose. . .

And so it all came out at last. Her helpless response to Paul's manipulation, her decision to go to Morocco with him and her mother's repudiation of her, her rapid loss of innocence about the relationship and her decision to end it.

It was scary to have to say it all, and she kept looking for the moment when he would look at her with distaste and dawning disappointment. But it didn't come. . . . Or perhaps he was simply too good at listening while hiding what he might really feel.

She pressed on, telling it as simply and as sensibly as she could—her belief, on Paul's return to Camberton, that she owed him another chance; her sincere attempts to find a meaning in her relationship with the gravely ill man, and her final realisation that she could not do it.

'And what I'm left with is a chasm between myself and my parents that may never be bridged.'

'You haven't tried?'

'No.' Her dismissal of the idea was too automatic and she knew that he would challenge it.

'Why don't you?' He was sitting on the desk in the corner of the room that was always a repository for piles of unfinished paperwork. He'd had to shift a stack of folders in order to find room there. Now he stood once again. 'It seems to me that you were prepared to give your relationship with Paul a second chance, but you won't do the same with your parents.'

'I'd made a commitment to Paul in my own mind. You've said yourself, Lee, how important you think it is that people stick things out in those circumstances. Find some forgiveness.'

'And there's no commitment to your parents? No capacity for forgiveness there? Just because there's no single moment at which a commitment is made doesn't mean it's any less strong. Write to them if you're afraid you'll say it all wrongly on the phone.'

She laughed helplessly. 'You make it sound easy.' Which it is for you, because you're not involved. That's gone between us now.

'No, not easy,' he told her slowly. 'Simple, though, and obvious. You feel bad about the estrangement—

therefore you should try to end it. Simple. . .but never easy. Funny, we tend to use those words as if they mean the same thing.'

'But you're right, they don't,' she nodded.

'Do you think you'll do it?'

'I—I'll try.'

'Let me know how it turns out.'

He didn't wait for an answer and his long strides took him from the room in seconds, leaving her alone to wonder wryly, 'Now, was that professional counselling or personal concern? It shouldn't matter to me. . .but it does!'

She wrote a letter to her parents that night.

CHAPTER TEN

THE summer heatwave continued well into the next week, oppressing Karen's spirits and dragging her deeper into doubt. She had written that letter to her parents in such a spirit of faith—the sort of 'act of faith' that Lee had talked about ten days ago in relation to Mark and Michael—and yet since posting it she had been full of pessimism and doubt. If Mum really meant what she said that day. . .

She wondered now, Is this why I feel so empty? Because I'm scared? Or is it just that I'm tired from the heat?

In her heart she knew that neither of those possibilities provided the full answer, but at least relief from the heat would come tonight in the air-conditioned cinema where she was seeing the second in a series of French comedy screenings with Susie. They were eating beforehand, too, in a small café, just along from the cinema, which served light evening meals.

Susie seemed to be feeling the heat as well. 'Where's my millionaire with the enormous kidney-shaped pool?'

'Swimming in it right now, I expect,' Karen returned, 'with a bevy of bathing beauties.'

'Yes, and every one of them a good nine inches taller than I am,' small Susie agreed.

She was 'starving' once again, having once again missed a meal during her morning shift, and moaned indecisively over the menu for several minutes while Karen, who had quickly decided on salad and a vege-tarian bake, stared idly out of the window.

It was good to have nothing to do, other than feel pleasantly hungry. Good to have some breathing space. Susie was always serenely oblivious to her friends' periods of emotional turmoil and wouldn't demand any kind of heart-to-heart, which was a relief, really. Karen knew that she'd been doing enough wallowing on her own, and didn't need encouragement from anyone else, thanks!

What is *wrong* with me?

A mocking Fate reminded her of the real answer all too forcefully just minutes later. Lee walked past the café window. It wasn't such a coincidence. He was, no doubt, doing exactly as she was—eating somewhere, then seeing the French film.

And his companion was Melody Piper, dressed— almost as she had been at the fair—in very tight white leggings and a billowing iridescent blouse that had fallen several inches off her shoulder. As Karen watched she adjusted the blouse, pulling it up onto her shoulder again so that now it draped low over her extravagant chest. She was holding Lee's arm, closely pressed to his side, and now she turned and looked up at him, nestled her head into his neck, touched his hair and pressed her full mouth against his lips.

And, while Lee might not have initiated or invited the moment, he certainly didn't seem to be shaking it off. They moved beyond Karen's range of vision now, and she assumed that they'd be eating at the rather more expensive French provincial restaurant several doors along. . .after they'd finished with that steamy kiss.

I'm falling in love with him and it's not going to go away.

The realisation ached in her bones like an illness, painful yet clearer than ever before.

This is what love is—this blend of friendship and safety and passion and instinct. But it's too late to know it now. The timing was wrong; I mucked it all up, and he's turned to Melody. . .

The waitress came to take their order and she intoned it mechanically after Susie had had a last-minute dither between chilled soup and spinach salad.

'Do you think I did the right thing?' she wanted to know a few minutes later, and Karen was completely at sea.

'About what?'

'The soup, of course. Should I have had the salad? Which will be more filling? Of course, then there's the savoury pancakes to come, but—'

'The soup will be fine.'

'Hmm. . .' Susie frowned and cast sceptical looks at the other meals she could see on nearby tables, as if suspecting that she'd been conned into ordering kitchen scraps.

Karen had to laugh.

'What?' her friend demanded suspiciously.

'Just you. And food.' It reminded her too much of Lee himself and that day at the fair which could so easily have been the beginning of something long and deep and magical, instead of just the brief flaring of a doomed spark.

Susie was uncowed by Karen's amusement. 'One of the few pleasures still within the means of the toiling masses.'

'And you're a toiling mass?' It was good to talk in this silly vein.

'Are you joking? A nurse?' Susie exclaimed. 'The *toilingest*, my dear! So don't try to strip all meaning from my life by suggesting I shouldn't enjoy my food.'

'I wasn't, I promise.'

But, meanwhile, what do I do to make this bearable? Leave Linwood?

No, not that. Not yet. Not when she craved Lee's

company, like craving some soothing, sensuous balm on raw, throbbing skin.

In the cinema, an hour later, she couldn't see him or Melody and wondered if she had been wrong about their plans for the evening, but then the lights dimmed and the previews of coming attractions began. A moment later she heard Melody's carrying, extravagantly modulated voice and her giggle along the aisle in the darkness.

'Oops, Lee, hold me! I'm blind in the dark. I have no night vision at all. I'll sit in someone's lap in a minute. . .'

There was an irate 'Shh!' from elsewhere in the cinema, and Melody subsided with a last giggle. Her silhouette and Lee's were unmistakable, though, when they finally found seats just two rows ahead and to the right of Karen.

She tried valiantly, but couldn't enjoy the film. Melody did, resting her head on Lee's shoulder every time she laughed at the antics on screen—as if to say, Isn't this just delicious! And, afterwards, when the credits began to roll she didn't show any inclination to move, so that Karen was able to get herself and Susie away without being seen.

Not a particularly triumphant achievement, under the circumstances.

It was another four days before the heatwave broke, and the growing expectation of a change hanging in the heavy air had weighed on Karen as a physical counterpoint to her expectancy each day when she looked at the mail or heard the phone ring in her flat. Mum and Dad must have received her letter by now, but they hadn't replied. Had Lee been wrong to urge her to write? Had she been wrong to trust his judgement so completely?

Karen spent a superficially pleasant weekend swimming and sunning herself with Susie, who was off for three days. Then, at last on Sunday night, thunder rolled overhead and the rain started. On Monday morning it was still raining and so much cooler that two of the staff and several patients at Linwood were heard to wonder aloud, with some regret, why they hadn't appreciated the heat and sunshine when they had it!

Still, the damp, chilly air was invigorating and Karen started her shift with a hard-headed determination to find time for several low-priority practical tasks, such as sorting out the lost property cupboard which had been neglected since. . .

Well, in the case of the lost property cupboard, she strongly suspected that it hadn't been tackled since Linwood first opened—over a year ago now. And as many of their elderly patients were rather prone to losing things without realising it—knitting, handkerchiefs, watches, jewellery and even their teeth—it really ought to be done, or at the very least delegated to someone else.

But, speaking of teeth. . . Karen thought as she crossed the main foyer at half past nine, shortly after the arrival of the day patients, Miss Gillis seemed to have lost hers.

She was a dear thing—eighty-eight years old, physically frail but with a satisfying sense of humour, a talent for making rather sharp, clever observations on modern life and a maddening tendency to click her false teeth rhythmically in and out of position in her mouth. At the moment, though, those teeth were definitely gone, and her mouth had caved in on itself to give her face the appearance of a nutcracker.

'What's happened to your teeth, Miss Gillis?' Karen asked cheerfully.

'She's late, but she'll be here soon,' came the firm but very inappropriate reply.

'No, Miss Gillis, I wasn't asking about Miss Marcie.' This was Miss Gillis's sprightly eighty-two-year-old sister, who delivered and fetched her on the bus with religious punctuality every day. 'I was asking about—'

'She'll be here soon,' Miss Gillis repeated.

'Oh, she will?' Karen abandoned the issue of the teeth for a moment. 'Are you going home, then?'

'Of course! I live at home. I don't live here. This place appears to be a hospital of some kind. And don't pretend you don't know it, because you're in a nurse's uniform yourself! Possibly it's a mental hospital. . .'

'No, it's not, Miss Gillis. It's Linwood, remember? You come here to day hospital. Miss Marcie brings you every day.'

The faded old eyes looked blank, and Karen's heart sank. Miss Gillis wasn't normally confused. Nor, in spite of clicking them so frequently, did she just leave her teeth lying about. Like her sister, she was neat and well organised. What had gone wrong?

Karen took her hand carefully, patted it and said, 'Never mind, we'll sort this out.' Then she found a pulse. A hundred and ten beats per minute, and irregular. Miss Gillis had had lumbar back pain for some years, apparently, but last week she had complained about it several times, saying it had got worse.

'We've got a new couch and it's not very comfortable,' was Miss Marcie's explanation, but Karen now felt less sure.

'Is your back hurting you?' she asked Miss Gillis now. 'Would you like to lie down?'

'Yes, that's a good idea.' She got readily—and unsteadily—to her feet, apparently forgetting her earlier belief that Miss Marcie was coming for her.

'And where are your teeth?' Karen asked once more.

'Oh, I had to have them out last week. I'm going to get some false ones.'

'I see. . .' The only problem here was that Miss Gillis had had to have her own teeth removed over thirty years ago.

Karen took her to the small room where day patients

could rest if they weren't feeling well and took her blood pressure, which came in at 140 over 80—higher than it should have been—then left her alone for a moment in order to check the patient history which was kept on file for each of their patients.

Miss Gillis was taking several medicines, including vitamin K to help slow the progress of her osteoporosis, but it didn't seem likely that any of these could be causing a problem.

'Much better lying down,' she told Karen a few minutes later.

'Can I feel your tum, Miss Gillis, for a moment?'

'Yes... This is a hospital, then, is it?'

'Yes, it's Linwood, Miss Gillis,' Karen repeated, gently palpating the old woman's abdomen. There was evidently some tenderness, but she couldn't feel any mass.

Difficult! She didn't really trust Miss Marcie's theory about the new couch. The morning, holding so much promise of productivity, was slipping by and she was tempted just to leave the elderly patient lying down for the day—especially since she seemed quite comfortable now.

But that fact in itself set off alarm bells. She wouldn't have thought that the back pain would ease so completely if it was due to muscle or joint stiffness and poor support.

Lee was usually in his office at this time of day. She was far too aware of his work habits and his timetables these days. It was hard to work with him so closely... and yet there was a pleasure in it, too, a sense of warmth, because as colleagues they got on as well as they always had.

On the surface, at least. She kept him well plied with humour, loving the sound of his laughter, and took pains to present the doings and problems of the patients in a way that would draw his interest. And she had the bitter satisfaction of knowing that he still enjoyed her company, no matter what the state of his relationship with the flamboyant and newly divorced Mrs Piper.

'I'm worried about Miss Gillis,' she told him straight away and he listened as he always did, taking the perceptions of his staff very seriously.

'You're worried it could be something internal?' He darkened the screen on his computer as he spoke.

'Yes, because symptoms of that sort of thing in the elderly are often less specific than they might be in a younger person, aren't they?'

'Want a second opinion?'

'If you've got time. She does seem quite comfortable now she's lying on her back, so perhaps it's nothing.'

'Or it could be something silent and serious. As you say, she's not normally confused which certainly indicates something.'

They walked together along the corridor and she was painfully conscious of his nearness, the warmth of his capable body, the defined rhythm of his stride—even his breathing. Conscious of her own body, too, and of a very foolish need to be closer to him—to feel his touch.

Miss Gillis was lying just as she had been left on the clean white sheeting of the bed, quite serene.

'No, it doesn't hurt now that I'm in hospital,' she said in answer to Lee's question. 'I expect. . . Did the doctor give me something? This is a nice place. What's it called? Where exactly am I?'

Then, when he palpated her abdomen as Karen had done, she frowned and winced. 'That doesn't feel very nice at all. . .'

Straightening, Lee drew Karen aside with a loose hold on her arm that she longed to lean into—longed to make a full embrace. He must have heard her slightly uneven breathing because he dropped his hold at once and she felt that she had impinged upon his body space in an unacceptable way.

'I'm going to send her to hospital,' he said, his words overriding the awareness between them, and his gold-flecked gaze was as steady and open as it always was. 'We may be making a fuss about nothing, but she's definitely not herself. Could you drive her up and arrange for her to be seen? I'll phone Miss Marcie and, meanwhile, one of our volunteers can go with you and sit with her until she's been seen or until her sister arrives.'

'Will you ring the hospital to say that we're coming?'

'I'm on my way. . .'

So the lost property cupboard didn't get done that morning after all although Miss Gillis's teeth were eventually found, resting tidily on top of a pile of magazines in the patients' lounge.

Karen was back at Linwood well before lunch, leaving Miss Gillis with a capable volunteer to wait for a doctor's examination. Then the pace picked up again. There were three new admissions, two discharges and two new day patients, and they required a lot of work—getting people settled; talking with patients' families; filling in forms and reports.

Then there were complaints about the lunch. It was chicken curry, which the Linwood kitchen staff didn't do well at the best of times, and today someone had had a heavy hand with the spices so that all the patients found it too hot to eat—except for Mr Shah, whose opinion was that the recipe was still terrible but at least today's was spicy enough to disguise the fact.

And as Karen was in the midst of frantic attempts to negotiate a last-minute alternative with the highly insulted head cook, even if it was only bread and cheese, she heard Melody Piper's unmistakable voice along the corridor and glimpsed her disappearing into Lee's office. 'I've brought the "R and J" budget, my love, and—

since I *know* you never take a proper break—a picnic lunch we can share all cosily in—'

Melody closed the office door behind her and Karen heard no more.

Lunch ended. Mr Makepeace had spilled curry all down his front—which was distinctly annoying since, like most of the others, he'd only eaten a single mouthful—and now he very stubbornly and loudly didn't want to change. There was a cupboard full of clean and well-cared-for second-hand clothing kept at Linwood for just this sort of eventuality, but some patients did object to the idea of wearing clothes that were not their own.

Karen didn't insist, just helped difficult Mr Makepeace to wipe himself down as best he could, and then everyone had to put up with the smell of a curry that no one had liked in the first place, providing a sensory accompaniment to the afternoon's film screening.

It happened, by pure coincidence, to be *A Passage to India*. Harry Makepeace thought this a great joke. 'Atmosphere! Perfect for the atmosphere! We'll all enjoy it twice as much now!' He was, unfortunately, quite alone in this opinion.

At half past three there was a ruthlessly efficient meeting with the therapy staff about plans for the coming month. Really, they couldn't have got through everything any quicker and yet it was still nearly twenty past four when it was over.

I don't know *how* I thought I'd get any extra jobs done today, Karen thought.

And she'd heard no news of Miss Gillis, she realised, remembering the first hitch in her optimistic schedule of this morning. Lee would know. . .and Melody must have gone by now, after their 'picnic'.

She hadn't, though. She was still sitting in his office pecking away on his typewriter. Karen glimpsed the heading 'Romeo and Juliet: Revised Production Budget', caught herself, appalled, in the bitchy thought that Melody's ensemble of diaphanous cream baby-doll dress over a skimpy black T-shirt—teamed with big black military boots—was much more appropriate to a rebellious sixteen-year-old than to a woman of over twice that age, and turned quickly to Lee to say, 'Sorry to bother you. . .'

'No bother.'

'. . .but I did want to hear about Miss Gillis before I leave.'

'My goodness, is it that late?' he exclaimed.

'Nearly half past four.'

'I'm almost done, love,' Melody squeaked. 'We said five hundred quid for publicity, didn't we?'

'Think so.' He frowned. 'But next time I won't believe you when you tell me you're a speedy typist.'

She giggled then said, not meaning it in the least, 'So-o-r-ry! Numbers and columns are tricky.'

'Now. . . The news on Miss Gillis,' Lee went on. 'Our suspicions were justified. Yours, I should say.'

He touched her briefly but she flinched at the contact, too afraid of what it might betray to Melody as well as to Lee himself. He noticed her reaction, of course, and she bit her lip, realising now that it was more telling than accepting the gesture would have been.

'The doctor who examined her ordered an X-ray and it showed the build-up of gas beneath the diaphragm from a perforated peptic ulcer that no one knew she had. It could have been extremely nasty if it hadn't been spotted.'

Karen agreed with a nod and a hiss of breath.

'As it is, she was sent straight into surgery. I'll phone tomorrow for more news.'

'Well, I'm glad, then,' Karen said. 'Not that it *was* a perforated ulcer, but that we didn't just send her off home with instructions to take aspirin and lie down.'

Melody shuddered at her typewriter, pecked out a few

more numbers and said, 'I don't know how you do it, Lee, I really don't!'

'Ah, Melody, no, you don't, do you?' he said, very ambiguously. Then to Karen, and perhaps it was a hint, 'Off home now, then?'

'Yes, which my feet will thank me for.'

There was another shudder from Melody. 'And then it all starts again, *exactly* the same, tomorrow at some ungodly hour, emptying bed pans and rubbing at your varicose veins.'

'Yes, that's right, and then I go home every night to my cheerless boarding-house to darn my stockings and wash my smalls in the sink, and make tea with the same water in which I boiled my solitary egg so as to save money on the gas meter,' Karen joked rather tartly.

'What? Making tea with——! Oh, you're not serious.'

'No, just completing your graphic sketch of a nurse's grim life.' And now Lee will hate me for being rude to his lover and thank his lucky stars that due to my murky timing over Paul he escaped an entanglement with such a vinegar-mouthed hag. . .

She got herself away after this, collected her bag from the staffroom and heard Melody's voice again behind Lee's closed office door, 'You see, Lee, getting out of nursing will help you to——'

Lee was getting out of nursing?

It might solve all my problems, Karen realised, because I'm not sure that I can go on working with him when I feel like this. I thought I could, but. . .

The writing leaped straight out at Karen from her post as she fanned through it, walking up the stairs to her flat that afternoon. Her mother's sloping hand, written in dark blue ink with her old green fountain-pen.

'At last! What took you so long, Mum? I'd given up. . .' she whispered.

Her hands were shaking and her eyes were already tear-blinded as she opened her door and fell clumsily inside, dropping her bag and the other unwanted items that the post had brought.

The envelope wouldn't unfasten easily and she began to tear it across the top, then realised that she was tearing the letter as well, so managed to rein herself in enough to go to the kitchen and get a knife. Slitting the creamy paper, she cut herself as well—a sharp, clean cut across her index finger that stung and needed ointment and a plaster at once. Not serious. Just annoying. Upsetting, too, with the delay it caused. It was deep enough that it would probably throb for the rest of the day.

Then, finally, the two closely-written pages were in her hand.

'Your letter came while we were away,' read the blue writing, and as she read it Karen could almost hear her mother's voice. 'I'm so sorry about the delay. You must have thought I'd torn it up and, if you *did* think that, I wouldn't blame you. I was so very wrong that day last October. I realised it almost at once, but by then you'd gone and I had no address. Your card from Morocco helped, but then no further word. I won't deny that I'm glad your relationship with Paul didn't last, but perhaps that's irrelevant now. If we've forgiven each other for that awful day, then nothing else matters.'

The letter went on, with paragraphs added by her father and greetings and love from her younger brothers, and after she had read it through twice Karen sat for a long time in silence on her couch, struggling with her feelings of hope and forgiveness and planning a trip to London as soon as possible. Finally, she thought about Lee and what he had done to encourage her.

I must thank him. I don't know how long I would have taken to get to this point if he hadn't urged me to, she thought, and the need to see him was so imperative and immediate that she would scarcely have allowed herself the time to change, except that her face was blotched from crying and the aura of cheap curry still clung to her uniform after today's events over lunch.

Fifteen minutes later, dressed in a floral cotton skirt and a matching top that fell straight to just below her waist and buttoned at the back, she rang a taxi and paced her flat as she waited for it, feeling the throb of her cut finger. Then she had to struggle to remember and describe to the driver the location of Lee's old farmhouse, so that she arrived there still in the first flush of her impulsive need to see him and had dismissed the taxi before she even thought to check that he was home . . . or that he was home alone.

Her purpose suddenly wavering, she remembered that she had seen him last with Melody who hadn't looked as if she were in much of a hurry to part from his company. They would probably go straight from Linwood to dinner. Or worse, perhaps she was here with him now.

She saw his car, parked in its spot beneath a run-down old arbour covered in glorious wisteria that served as a garage, and she almost fled. I shouldn't have come. I could have found a moment to thank him tomorrow at work just as well. If I walk home . . .

But then he opened the door before she could take another step.

'I heard the taxi. Come in.' His tall, rangy figure almost filled the low doorway, then he stood back to let her through, and she felt his warmth cloak her briefly as she brushed past.

'Are you . . . alone?' She couldn't bear to ask straight out if Melody was there—to betray her pointless jealousy in such a way. The house seemed quiet as he led her through to the old farm kitchen, mellow and warm in the late afternoon light which streamed through parting clouds. The kettle was just beginning to sing on the Aga.

'Quite alone,' he answered her cheerfully. 'Even the dog is at the vet.'

'Oh, how is he. . .?'

'He's fine. And you haven't come to ask about my dog. . .have you?' He switched off the kettle.

'No. I heard from my mother today.'

'Oh, Karen. . .'

'A long letter in the post. Everything's fine. They'd been away. So I came to thank you.'

'No need,' he said briefly, and she couldn't help wondering if it was a dismissal, but then he went on rather slowly, 'I've been waiting, actually, and when you didn't say anything I was afraid it hadn't worked out and you might be angry.'

'*Angry*?'

'At my interference. At my high-handed advice.' He spread his hands. 'If I'd misjudged the situation it could have made things even worse.'

'Misjudged? No!' she argued fervently, stepping closer to him and not caring, for a moment, what he might be thinking of her. 'You have such a gift for healing, Lee— healing rifts between people; finding the right solution. You seem to know by instinct when something's important.'

'Do I?' he smiled wryly, turning away a little. 'Kind of you to say so, but I wonder. . .'

The mood of self-doubt was so unlike his normal aura of quiet confidence that she cast him a sharp glance which he caught. His laugh was short and rather harsh as he answered her unworded question. 'Well, I was wrong about us, wasn't I? I was quite sure that that was going to be important.' He began to pace the kitchen, as if caged by its walls.

'No, hell!' he amended harshly. 'It was *already* important, but then when you refused to talk to me about what was holding you back it seemed obvious that I didn't count much with you at all.' He laughed again but with anger, not with amusement.

'Oh, no, that's not how it was, Lee,' Karen told him, feeling very wooden, as if she were speaking disinterestedly of something that had happened a long time ago. The bitterness which had surfaced suddenly in his tone was hard to take. She stared at the bandaged cut on her hand, unwilling to meet his regard while she was giving so much away.

'Actually, it was *because* you counted that I couldn't tell you about Paul. I was so afraid, you see, that I'd lose your respect and certainly anything else you might have started to feel.'

'You're far too hard on yourself.' His words seemed like just a distant, rational commentary. 'Your relationship with Paul was a mistake, sure, but do you think I've never made one? Did you really think I couldn't forgive a mistake?'

'Perhaps,' she acknowledged with a tiny nod, then went on, 'But then when I realised I couldn't rekindle a relationship with him I felt that at least I owed it to him to tell him first. You were angry, and I understand, and after that it was. . .too late for us, don't you think? Not too late for us as friends, I hope, but as lovers. The timing has been so wrong, for both of us, and I can't blame you for losing interest. And for having moved on,' she finished firmly, thinking of Melody.

'Moved on? What the hell do you mean by that?'

She was so startled at the challenging bluntness of the question that she just blurted out. 'You're involved with Melody Piper now, aren't you?'

He snorted and shook his head, incredulous. 'Involved with Melody?' He was facing her now, with the golden light behind his head as it streamed through the window, and she couldn't read his face or his voice at all any more.

'I—I saw you kissing her at the French film.' It

sounded horribly like a jealous accusation.

His eyes had narrowed, and she went on quickly. 'I—You didn't see me. It was dark when the two of you arrived. I was there with Susie. It was hard not to see that Melody was, well, all over you.'

'Like a red rash,' he agreed easily and not unkindly. 'And you didn't notice that I was no more all over her than sheer politeness demanded? She's just divorced, very emotional and casting about for a new man. Most misguidedly, she's picked me; wants me to give up nursing and apply for the job of administering the Camberton Theatre Company, so that I'm more suitable as her partner. It's out of the question and she'll soon realise it. So does that get Melody out of this mess?'

'Yes, OK. I'm sorry if I sounded. . . But you can't blame me for—'

'I can't blame you for suggesting that our timing is less than stellar, sure,' he growled, studying her. Aware of the intensity of his scrutiny, she couldn't look up at all. Her vision was blurred and it was hard even to take in his next words. 'But if I can wade my way through this mess to what really counts, it seems that we're both. . .' he laughed once more '. . .still interested.'

'Interested. . .?' she echoed dazedly.

'Yes! Interested!' he bit out, striding ominously to within inches of her and glaring into her face—forcing her to meet his eyes. 'You know, Karen! Set alight when someone comes into the room; curious about every detail in their life; aware of them with every pore in your skin; happy when you're with them, restless and numb and bored when you're not. "Interested." It's a boring word with a magical definition. Does it apply in this case, or not?'

'Well, it applies to me,' she returned meekly, her heart beginning to race, 'but I didn't think that you—'

She wasn't permitted to finish. 'Oh, God, Karen,' Lee

said against her lips. 'Bad timing isn't the end of everything. I've had nothing *but* bad timing in my relationships
in the past, and I've let each one slide because the timing
made me realise it wasn't the right one. This time I'm
not giving in and that says something, don't you think?
Are you going to let one false start defeat you? I'm not!
Not with you! Can't we start again. . .with *this*. . .' he
drank at her mouth, then breathed fire against her ear
'. . .and follow it as far as we dare? We *must*, Karen!
Feel me! When I'm shaking like this, don't you think
we must?'

'Yes, oh. . .yes!'

She arched herself passionately against him and felt
his heat swamp her as his arms tightened around her.
His kiss deepened until she was completely lost in it and
she felt that she never wanted it to end.

Letting his eyes drift open, Lee saw the intensity of
her abandonment through the mist of his lashes and his
heart turned over. She was small in his arms, small and
strong and steadfast, and when he thought about how
close they had come to not getting this right it made his
insides crumble in fear.

He'd always believed in the power of small beginnings
and now he had to start believing in the power of difficult
beginnings—bad ones, unlikely ones—beginnings that
almost became endings without a pause for breath or
pleasure in between.

And this still *was* a beginning, he knew. With her
past—and, despite his real belief that she should put it
behind her, he loved her for the way she took even a
mistaken commitment seriously—it would take both of
them time to get this thing to the place he wanted it to be.

For now. . .

'I like this blouse,' he murmured, and let his hands
slip beneath it to cover her bare skin with a questing
touch as he splayed his fingers across her back then

brought them round very slowly to nudge at her gratify-
ingly swollen breasts, 'but how does it, um—? Ah!'

He found the buttons at the back and began to slip them
undone, pausing halfway only long enough to switch
attention to the fastening of her bra and unclip that as
well. Slipping both garments off her shoulders a minute
later, he looked at her creamy fullness for the first time
and took a shuddering breath. 'I've wanted so badly to—'

'Oh, I know. I know, now. And I have, too.'

For quite a long time they didn't touch at all, then he
reached out a hand to brush against the tightly furled bud
of her nipple and she gasped then moaned as at last he
took her fully in his arms and left a trail of kisses from
her mouth to her throat, and down, and down. . .

'Karen, is it too soon to take you to bed?' he asked
in a low voice at last.

He hadn't planned to say this. With all that sober
musing about beginnings he'd thought of waiting but
now the words had simply spilled from his hungry lips
of their own accord and he held his breath, waiting—
having to tighten every muscle in his body to stop himself
from trembling.

'No, it's not too soon. . .' came her firm, whispered
answer, and so he literally took her, lifting her into his
arms and carrying her to his still sun-lit bedroom for a
night of achingly sweet discovery.

They were married five months later and that, she whispered to him at the altar after their vows were made and
he had lifted her creamy veil to reach her mouth, was
the best beginning of all.

MILLS & BOON®
Medical Romance™

COMING NEXT MONTH

MISLEADING SYMPTOMS by Lilian Darcy
Camberton Hospital

How could Dr Megan Stone work with Dr Callum Priestley again, when she couldn't forget the night they had shared two years previously? Callum behaved as if nothing had happened, but now Megan really wanted him to see her as more than a colleague...

OUTLOOK—PROMISING! by Abigail Gordon
Springfield Community Hospital

Dr Rachel Maddox needed a quiet life after her divorce, and her new job and home seemed ideal—until Nicholas Page, eminent neuro-surgeon, began involving her in his life, and trying to organise hers!

HEART SURGEON by Josie Metcalfe
St Augustine's Hospital

Sister Helen Morrisey's sole aim was to be part of surgeon Noah Kincaid's team, because only then did she have a chance of regaining her small son from the Middle East. But she'd forgotten something important, and Noah offered to smooth her path—but what did he gain?

SISTER SUNSHINE by Elisabeth Scott
Kids & Kisses

Widower Dr Adam Brent was sure Sister Julie Maynard wouldn't cope with the job, but she proved him wrong, charming the patients, his two small children—and Adam! But he still wasn't prepared for commitment...

MILLS & BOON®

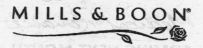

Marry me COWBOY

When your lover is a cowboy...

**You'll have a stetson on the bedpost
and boots under the bed.**

**And you'll have a man who's hard-living,
hard-loving and sexy as hell to keep you warm
all night...every night!**

Watch it happen in these four delightful new stories
by your favourite authors—
Janet Dailey,
Margaret Way, Susan Fox and Anne McAllister

Available: May 1997   Price: £4.99

MILLS & BOON®

To HAVE & TO HOLD

Celebrate the joy, excitement and sometimes mishaps that occur when planning that special wedding in our treasured four-story collection.

Written by four talented authors—
Barbara Bretton, Rita Clay Estrada,
Sandra James and Debbie Macomber

Don't miss this wonderful short story collection for incurable romantics everywhere!

Available: April 1997   Price: £4.99

KEEPING COUNT

How would you like to win a year's supply of Mills & Boon® books? Well you can and they're FREE! Simply complete the competition below and send it to us by 31st October 1997. The first five correct entries picked after the closing date will each win a year's subscription to the Mills & Boon series of their choice. What could be easier?

$$6 \; + \; 3 \; + \; \Box \; = \; 14$$

$$\Box \; + \; 2 \; + \; \Box \; = \; 15$$

$$\Box \; + \; 1 \; + \; \Box \; = \; 16$$

$$\Box \; + \; 6 \; + \; \Box \; = \; 17$$

$$\Box \; + \; 3 \; + \; \Box \; = \; 18$$

$$\Box \; + \; 1 \; + \; \Box \; = \; 19$$

$$\Box \; + \; 5 \; + \; \Box \; = \; 20$$

C7D

PLEASE TURN OVER FOR DETAILS OF HOW TO ENTER ☞

How to enter...

There are six sets of numbers overleaf. When the first empty box has the correct number filled into it, then that set of three numbers will add up to 14. All you have to do, is figure out what the missing number of each of the other five sets are so that the answer to each will be as shown. The first number of each set of three will be the last number of the set before. Good Luck!

When you have filled in all the missing numbers don't forget to fill in your name and address in the space provided and tick the Mills & Boon® series you would like to receive if you are a winner. Then simply pop this page into an envelope (you don't even need a stamp) and post it today. Hurry, competition ends 31st October 1997.

Mills & Boon 'Keeping Count' Competition
FREEPOST, Croydon, Surrey, CR9 3WZ

Eire readers send competition to PO Box 4546, Dublin 24

Please tick the series you would like to receive if you are a winner
Presents™ ❏   Enchanted™ ❏   Temptation® ❏
Medical Romance™ ❏   Historical Romance™ ❏

Are you a Reader Service Subscriber?   Yes ❏   No ❏

Ms/Mrs/Miss/Mr_____

(BLOCK CAPS PLEASE)

Address _____

_____

_____ Postcode_____

(I am over 18 years of age)

One application per household. Competition open to residents of the UK and Ireland only.
You may be mailed with other offers from other reputable companies as a result of this application. If you would prefer not to receive such offers, please tick box. ❏

C7D